SHATTERED PATHS

DANIEL ROLPH

To every child who has endured trauma.
Your strength, your story, and your journey matter. This is for you and the
resilience you carry with you each and every day.

FOREWORD

Shattered Paths is not just a story—it's a reflection of my life growing up in the UK care system. As a child, I experienced the highs and lows of foster care, and these books are my way of giving a voice to those children who, like me, felt invisible and unheard.

However, Shattered Paths is more than a tale of foster care. It's a story about resilience, identity, and survival—universal themes that resonate with anyone who has faced hardship. While the focus may be on childhood trauma, rejection, and the fight to belong, I believe that most of us, at some point in our lives, have navigated our own challenges.

Through these stories, I aim not only to shed light on the often-overlooked realities of foster care and childhood trauma but also to connect with anyone who has ever felt lost, rejected, or misunderstood. My hope is to encourage reflection and start conversations about the inner strength that carries us through life's hardest moments.

SHATTERED PATHS

1

How long do you think five quid could stretch on an empty stomach? No, not just an empty stomach but an empty soul. I found out after standing on the steps of the latest foster care home from which the police escorted me. Five quid...that's what they handed me to go and find myself something to eat before dumping me off at some ramshackle B&B in one of the rougher parts of town.

Sitting in the back of the police car, I spent the ride looking out of the window at a cityscape I barely saw, the disjointed feeling of another home falling by the wayside overwhelming my brain. I didn't see it as a failure per se, but it definitely hit home in a way that felt all too familiar. The police radio would occasionally break the silence, but neither of the cops bothered to acknowledge me. To them, I was nothing more than a quick job between six and seven that evening, for which they'd most likely type up a quick report at the end of their shift before moving on with their lives.

I expected one of them to let me know that everything would be OK, to show just a little bit of empathy. They may not have seen me as a kid, and I may not have looked like one anymore, but that didn't change the fact I was still just fifteen. Imagine sitting in the back of a cop car as it pulled up to your new potential home without anybody giving you some sort of reassurance.

"Alright, grab your stuff, kid," one of them said as the car came to a stop in front of some nondescript building. The voice sounded indifferent, the tone more impatient than earlier. For all I knew, I could have been the last job of the day for the two, and all that stood between them and a cold beer was some annoying little twat needing an escort. "Come on, let's go, let's go," Impatient Cop repeated when I didn't move fast enough. I did as he asked, grabbed what little belongings I had, and climbed out.

Aside from some clothes, the only thing I had walking into the place was a second bag holding my food, the food I had managed to buy with that single fiver. The questionable people standing near the entrance and then the two halfway down the corridor all stared at my bag. I didn't have a doubt in my mind that if it weren't for the cops flanking me on either side, one of them would have grabbed it, probably even eaten the burger and chips in front of me just to ram home the suffering a little more.

That five quid barely lasted more than the time it took me to consume that first meal, a meal I barely remember eating, thanks to my overstimulated senses. Imagine sitting in a strange room all alone at just fifteen years of age and trying to understand the circumstances surrounding yet another shift in a string of relocations involving multiple homes and carers. Nobody would come and save me. Nobody would sit on the bed beside me, put their arm around my shoulders, and promise that everything would be OK.

If it hadn't been for the stale tobacco stink using the underlying aroma of dampness for support, I might not have felt as rejected by society the way I did that dark and miserable night. It didn't take long for the place to go back to normal once the officers left me to my own devices. Out in the hall, I could hear what can only be described as the world's loudest drug deal between some random user and my nearest neighbor, only fueling my fear even more. It wasn't exactly terror I felt, maybe something more akin to dread. I just about jumped out of my skin when someone knocked on my door and then held my breath when a gravelly woman's voice spoke through it.

"You want some special company for an hour, honey?"

That was the moment when I knew I was really alone...the first time in a long time that I couldn't point at someone else to deflect the attention away. It was while listening to that prostitute's hoarse proposition that I understood just how far down into the gutter my life had fallen this time. This was where the rejects lived...those society turned a blind eye to, and I had just become one of them.

The truth is, and I want you to know that I'm going to be as honest as possible in telling you my sordid tale, that everyone has a breaking point. The only question is when and how. For me, sitting in that darkened room did more than remind me of my place in the world. It brought the past few years back in a way that maybe should have stomped on what little remained of my soul.

I'd cried myself to sleep many times during my childhood, but that night wasn't one of them. I think I would have given anything to escape the room, if only into the confines of my unconscious mind, but fate had other ideas. I think it wanted me to listen to the drug dealer selling his wares along the corridor or the prostitutes trying to earn their next hit in one room or another.

I didn't have a watch, so I could only guess the time, but at some point, well after midnight, a fight broke out a few doors down from my own. Sleep had been teasing me from a distance, and I'd managed to close my eyes for a few seconds, but what little distance I fell into the depths of sleep quickly faded away when some sort of glassware struck a distant wall. It shattered into a thousand pieces before two voices began screaming at each other, the venomous insults of both the man and the woman rolling out with slurred conviction.

Already lying in a fetal position on the bed, I pulled my knees in even tighter, continuing to stare at the bright light from the hallway leaking around the edges of my door. Every now and then, the light would fade as some unseen person passed by, their shoes clicking on the hardwood floors with distinct echoes. The couple continued fighting, their screaming match occasionally interrupted by shouts from a nearby neighbor calling for them to shut the hell up. That then led the couple to turn their vocals on them before returning to whatever they were arguing over.

More crashing echoed through the walls as the screaming intensified, and I sat upright with my back against the wall. Looking over to the room's only window, I contemplated the possibility of using it to make my escape if I had to, but that was when I saw the familiar flashing of red and blue lights bouncing off my ceiling.

Despite my bladder screaming for me to give it some relief, I'd held on for God knows how long while battling my own inner demons, but seeing those familiar colours gave me a kind of reprieve. Leaving the safety of the bed for the first time in hours, I carefully walked to the window and stole a view of the two police cars parked outside the building. Almost at the same time, I heard solid boot heels echoing down the hallway before a sharp rap on a door brought what felt like the entire building to silence.

Holding both my breath as well as the pressure down below, I listened as an authoritative voice called out to whoever was in the apartment where the fight had taken place. I pictured those in adjoining apartments to also be standing in a near-identical posture to my own, the majority of crimes within the building briefly pausing while the law was around.

Not surprisingly, the cops began beating on the door, insisting someone open up, and when I heard one of the previous fighters call for the police to go away, I knew this wasn't going to end well. My left leg began jiggling uncomfortably as I realized the muscles holding in my pee were about to let go, and not wanting to add to my misery, I made a mad dash for the toilet. I'd barely got my zipper down before the shouting out in the hallway exploded all over again, this time with two new voices thrown in.

I had never focused on peeing as much as I did at that moment, trying to keep the stream steady while listening to the confrontation happening just a short way from my front door. The voices were briefly muffled a bit more from what I assumed to be the officers making their way into the apartment, but there was no denying the words.

"PUT IT DOWN NOW," one of them cried out over the top of a wall of abuse. The same man and woman seemed to have joined forces, their shouts aggressively filling the air before a scream suddenly rose above all else.

I'd never heard gunshots in real life before, not as close as they were that early morning, anyway. Each one echoed through the building with a thunderous boom, the accompanying screams filled with bloodcurdling angst. Chills rolled through me, the goosebumps breaking out across my skin as I instinctively ducked with each shot. By the third, my knees hit the floor, and I rolled onto my side for fear of a stray bullet blasting through the wall.

More police cars turned up within seconds, although this time accompanied by both lights and sirens, the latter cut off as each screeched to a halt beside the others. I was back at the window by then, an unseen bystander witnessing the next day's front-page news. Inside the building, the screams turned to both commands and sobbing, the woman throwing in a few abusive shouts whenever she took a deep breath. One of her outbursts happened directly out the front of my room, and I again jumped when someone smacked the door on their way past.

That night was my introduction to 177 Mackenzie Road, Brixton, an address not only associated with several high-profile news stories in years to come but also my home for the subsequent three months. Known as the Bucket by locals and residents alike, it served as a halfway house for recently released inmates from nearby Brixton Prison, and that in itself should be enough to explain the situation I'd been dropped in. The prison held a mix of mental health patients, substance abusers, and those convicted of a variety of sexual offences, not the kind of reformed prisoners a fifteen-year-old wanted to be hanging around with.

The laneway flanking the Bucket was known as Shooters Alley, and not only for the large number of locals who used the dark laneway for consuming their recently purchased drugs via various methods. During my three months, four murders took place within the space of five weeks, and all of them in the dead of night. I remember spending hours watching the cops and medics going in and out of the alley, their blue and red flashers illuminating the night.

The scary bit is that my time at the Bucket wasn't the worst part of this story, not by a long way. For you to get a real understanding of what I endured, we have to go back a few years. We need to go back to when a frightened kid found himself ripped from a kind of existence few would have seen as normal, and yet I found it to be my life. Those were the days before the horrors of the Thatchers, the Buxtons, and the permanent scars those months and years left on my soul.

While many might jump forth to defend the system entrusted to care for those who have nowhere else to turn, I'm willing to bet that the majority of those people didn't suffer the way those caught up in the bureaucratic red tape did. I'd be willing to bet that a lot of those people defending the system didn't have to spend days and weeks with complete strangers, enduring every kind of abuse imaginable, and left with the kind of trauma requiring lifelong therapy.

As I sit here writing these words, I find my fingers trembling, not because of the cold that's biting into me but because of the memories I've locked away into the darkest recesses of my mind. It's those very shadows that frighten me the most and the places I must open if I'm going to share the brutal reality of my time caught up in a system meant to protect me. Not just me but thousands of others.

For years, I tried my best to keep these memories hidden from the world. I think, in a way, I felt that not remembering meant that they would simply disappear into the passage of time and, with it, my scars. I was wrong. These stories need to be told for the names of those I met along the way to once again come to share a part of my life. It's also a chance for those lost to again feel the light of day upon their faces as I share the harrowing details behind the headlines announcing their departure.

I look at the tip of my pen as it hovers an inch above the paper and wonder where to begin. If I'm going to make you understand the horror, I first have to walk you through the corridors of time that brought the three of us together, the kids who found a sliver of hope in a system that almost broke the lot of us. It is there I still sometimes find myself now, back when I first saw the friends who would ultimately help me survive.

2

The only person who I can ever remember telling me genuinely that they loved me was my mum, a woman whose face has almost disappeared into the shadows of time. If I close my eyes and really try to think hard, I can still remember the moment, back when I was about four or five, and she was waiting for me at the bottom of a slide. I remember sitting on the very edge of the descent, a drop of only a couple of feet but looking like a cliff to a young kid. She stood at the bottom, hands held out, ready to catch me, with that warming smile only a mother could give.

The only thing that little boy sitting on the edge of that great precipice knew was that the woman waiting for him below loved him. Not only loved him, but she was also ready to protect him at any cost. He knew that if he pushed himself off, she would catch him at the other end, save him from hurtling off the edge and landing on the ground below where the danger always loomed. To a five-year-old, that was all that mattered.

What that little boy *didn't* know at the time, and something he wouldn't find out until years later, was that those random trips to the local playground weren't quite so random. That little boy didn't see the impatient foot tapping on the ground, the way his mother looked around at the different entrances of the park while waiting for her dealer. He didn't recognize the track marks on her arms, the shaking fingers, the withering body. The empty pantry, the lack of food, none of that stood out because, for him, those things were considered normal. When he asked for food, she gave it to him. When he needed a drink, she gave him a cup of water. All he knew was that warm and friendly smile looking back at him, the promise that she would always be there to catch him if he fell...right up until the day she wasn't.

Death isn't something a five-year-old can truly comprehend, so when I was told that my mother died three days before my sixth birthday, I had no clue as to what it actually meant. Sure, I knew that she wasn't coming back. She'd gone to heaven. The woman in the business suit told me so. But the more I asked when she would come back, the more irritated that woman became, her answers shorter and more to the point each time. Never wasn't a word I could quite get my head around, and if she was in heaven, then that meant she was *somewhere*, and if she was *somewhere*, then surely she'd find her way home again.

The other thing I couldn't understand was why I had to pack a suitcase with my things. That same woman, who I learned later to be a social services case worker assigned to my situation, kept telling me that I was going on a nice trip away, on a holiday, to be with other kids. I couldn't grasp why I couldn't just stay home; the idea that there would be no grown-up to care for me was still out of my reach.

What I do remember from the day I left the only home I'd ever known with just a small suitcase was that I had to leave without either my favourite teddy bear, Bob, or my best friend, Nate. Despite what I was being told, I had no way of understanding that this was a brand new life I was heading out to, one lacking the kind of comfort and security I'd been used to.

I still remember screaming when I reached the front door and the woman named Ingrid telling me to say goodbye. Up until that moment, I think there had still been the belief that I was only going for a night or two, that I would be brought back and allowed to continue living in my home. To have that woman's hands grab my arm and drag me through the front door felt foreign to me, and for another woman to then come and help the first made it even worse. I don't remember her face too well, the tears playing tricks with my vision. I watched the house through the back window of the car as we drove away for the final time, screaming for my mum to help me, to come and save me from the bad people. It was the first plea she ever failed to answer.

I went back to that house many years later and found nothing but an empty lot with overgrown weeds sprouting from what little remained of my childhood home. At the time of my departure, though, with a young mind devoid of any sort of life experience, it felt like my world had come to an end, and nasty people were kidnapping me into another. Fear, terror, all the feelings I couldn't verbalize took hold and didn't release their grip for a long time to come.

As strange as it may sound, I don't remember much else from that day other than the echoes. Maybe some of the flashes of memories fit in with that moment in time, but I can't be sure. Time is a curious thing, and it can play tricks on one's recollections. There was this chair they made me sit in after arriving at some building, a seat in a dark hallway. The woman went inside an office, and from there, I heard voices loud enough for them to echo down the corridor. I don't remember how long I sat there for, but at some point, I ended up back in the car and eventually found myself being walked to the front door of a home.

I don't remember ever being taken to the bedroom, where I ultimately fell asleep, but I do remember waking the next morning, that overwhelming sense of confusion gripping me hard. The bed I'd been put into was the bottom of a bunk bed located next to a window. When I initially sat up and looked out into the early morning, the only thing I could see was the brick wall of the building next door. Unable to recognize a single thing and sensing the presence of others in the room, I did what any other near-six-year-old would...I began to cry.

It's funny the things you forget and the things you always remember. Like, I don't remember the colour of the car that brought me to the Lightman's home, and yet I will always remember the morning I first met Norman Green, the kid who just happened to be sleeping in the bed above mine. The second I began to cry, he slid down off the top bunk, stood in front of me and just stared for a bit. A second later, bam, he punched me square in the face, pain exploding in my nose as thick mucus ran over my lips.

"Shut the hell up," he mumbled angrily before climbing back into his bed.

As blood and snot ran from both nostrils, I remember sitting there frozen, too scared to move. It hadn't been a gentle tap or the kind of half-arsed slap my mum used to give me when she was mad. This was a definitive, white-knuckle punch to the face that shut me up in an instant. The tears spilling down my cheeks weren't due to any sobbing but rather because of the burning heat emanating from the bridge of my nose.

That was my initial introduction to not only Norman Green and the Lightmans' Home for Disadvantaged Children but also to the system itself, a system that should have been looking after me instead of dumping me at the first open door it could find. Sitting in that bed, properly bleeding for perhaps the first time in my life, I understood that playtime was over. The age of survival had just begun, and if I was going to make it, I'd have to learn fast.

After another considerable spell of sitting silently in the middle of the bed, someone else suddenly stirred across from me. I heard a yawn before a rogue hand shot out from under a blanket, and then a face finally peered out and just stared out at me.

"We got a new kid last night," a voice spoke before more faces appeared from other beds.

Eight others, all boys, in four bunk beds, lived in the same room as me. There were two girls living in a bedroom next to mine, but I didn't see them often. Meal times were about it, and then only if we happened to be in the kitchen at the same time. You see, it wasn't like the movies or TV shows where we all had to sit around a great big table for meals. The Lightmans didn't even *own* a kitchen table big enough to fit us all. What they did have was a bench where the food would be left after the adults first helped themselves. Whatever remained is what the rest of us got to fight over, and fight over it we did.

Being the eldest, Norman got the most, usually grabbing the best of everything and sometimes filling his plate enough to empty the serving dish. A couple of the others might complain, but he'd just punch them away with little effort. Everybody knew to keep their distance. At sixteen, Norman was also the eldest of us, a clear two years older than both Pete and Rick. Me being the youngest meant everybody else would just shove me aside, which meant that some nights, I'd go hungry. So, why didn't I complain or just ask for more?

This wasn't a fictional story from yesteryear about a boy asking for more, but it certainly felt similar to that classic tale. To understand my surroundings, it might pay for me to explain to you the Lightmans in a little more detail. You see, the couple who welcomed random kids off the street weren't doing so for the love. You might assume that they had a special place in their heart for kids like me, opening their door to those in need of family and security and whatever else someone might hope for within a family environment. No, the Lightmans did it for one simple reason...money.

Money is what makes the world go 'round, isn't it? It took me about a day to understand the reality, even without anybody telling me so. It was the so-called father, a beast of a man named Patty Lightman, who unknowingly educated me. Born in Ireland, he spoke with an accent so thick that I barely understood him those first few days, and the best way to understand him was to listen to the tone and volume of his words. He'd swing a meaty hand at anybody who walked close to him and always called us his *walkin' pound notes*.

"Look at 'em, luv," he'd tell his wife while watching us trudge past. "Our little walkin' bills." I could imagine him seeing us as nothing more than fifty-pound notes walking back and forth. Maybe it wasn't him trying to swing at us. Perhaps he was trying to grab his fifty-pound notes.

He also smoked like a chimney, drank Guinness like a fish, and always disappeared for hours on end when he went *"Out wit da lads,"* as he used to tell Becky, not coming home some nights until well after midnight. Those were the nights when it was best to pull the pillow tight over your face to block out the fighting, husband and wife going at it for what felt like hours. Crockery smashing, the shouting, furniture tossed aside. It all added to the misery of those too young to fully comprehend just how shit we had it.

Those first few days were the hardest for me. I'd cop a punch to the face or arms from Norman whenever I cried or a backhanded slap from anybody else standing nearby. I learnt fast not to show emotion out in the open and held it in until the only time of the day or night when I knew I was truly alone...in bed after lights out. It was while lying in the darkness that I used my pillow like a shield, holding it over my face as I sobbed as quietly as I could. It was those first few long nights crying myself to sleep when I recalled my mother's smile gazing back at me from the shadows, trying to comfort me with a voice that felt a million years ago.

About a week after arriving at the Lightmans' house, my brief routine took another turn when I found myself sent off to the local school along with four of the other boys, each a couple of years or more older than me. Before you imagine some heartwarming scene of the four of us walking together as a group, let me quickly dispel that myth by sharing the actual truth. Only two out of the five walked together; the rest of us spread out, with dozens of yards between us. I, as usual, always brought up the rear, the rest of them too ashamed to be considered even remotely related to me.

The thing is, school became something of an escape for me, a place where a slither of normality drew me in. I still didn't fit in with the rest of the kids, of course, the sheer sight of my worn clothes and unkempt hair enough to keep the masses away. If I remember correctly, I don't think even the teachers gave me much of a break, the majority coming down harder on those who they knew to be *wardens of the state,* supposedly cared for by those looking for a quick cash reward. All but Mrs. Henry, of course. She was sweet, with a twinkle in her eye every time she shared a story with a happy ending.

No, it wasn't anybody in particular that felt like a reprieve for me at school, but more like the place itself. For the most part, it gave me a chance to blend in with the rest of the kids, disappearing into a sea of other faces. It was during those hours that I avoided doing anything that might highlight me. No raising my arm to answer a question willingly or volunteering for any of the requested duties. Most days, I doubt anybody would have noticed me at all if it weren't for the roll call. But then, no matter how much I wished the school day would go on forever, even *it* eventually betrayed me and back to the home I went.

And that's how it began for me, this life of living in homes with strangers who neither cared nor wanted me. It was a harsh reality for sure, and one I had to pick up in a hurry if I wanted to save myself beatings and whatnot. What I didn't know during those early weeks and months was that things could get even worse, and soon enough, they did.

3

While I guess you could say that the next few weeks took on a kind of routine, there were rare intermittent moments of sunshine. It wasn't all doom and gloom, although at times, it did feel quite overwhelming to think that I had no friends in this world. It wasn't until the arrival of a new foster child that my life became somewhat more bearable.

When Ritchie Blanton came to the Lightman home in the late summer of that year, he did so with a bang...an *actual* bang. Despite being a year younger than Norman, he stood almost a whole foot taller than him and the first run-in between the two left the older kid sitting on his butt with such a shocked look on his face. The rest of us, or at least those in the room at the time, watched on in stunned silence, too scared to move at the prospect of having a second bully living amongst us.

The fight, if you can call a one-punch exchange a fight, happened because Ritchie had dropped his bedding on one of the lower beds next to mine. Norman, feeling the urge to show whose house it was, swiped the bundle onto the floor before folding his arms across his chest. Ritchie barely paused, the punch barely visible but with enough power to send the older kid stumbling back a couple of steps before he lost his balance and fell. Just like I'd experienced a few weeks earlier, courtesy of the person now licking his wounds, Norman sat in silence while bleeding from his nose. Ritchie took a step forward and stared down at him.

"You got a problem?"

Norman's usually stern look evaporated, his white cheeks flushed with a crimson red that stretched all the way to the tips of his ears. For a second, it looked as if he might give in to the tears, but then I remembered the brilliant flash of pain from a similar punch, causing my own eyes to water profusely. He shook his head and then, within the blink of an eye, pushed himself off the floor and ran from the room. The rest of us held our places, not sure whether to follow our older brother, but that was when something remarkable happened. Ritchie looked around the room at each of us in turn and then said something I'll never forget.

"We already have enough shit to deal with without arseholes like that adding to it."

He didn't wait for a response. He just knelt down, picked up his bedding and began to make his bed. Once done, he grabbed a book from his bag, lay down and began to read. And just like that, we went from having to watch ourselves from an overzealous roommate to one who might have actually protected us from one.

The others left Ritchie alone for the most part. I heard Pete and Eugene whispering about him to one another while walking to school about how he seems like a loner since he never talked to anybody but I knew that not to be true. I don't know why, but I'd spoken to him a couple of times, once when I asked him what book he was reading and he held it up to show me.

"Count of Monte Cristo," he said before studying me a little closer. "How old are you, kid?"

"Six," I said, and I remember him grinning at me in a way I hadn't seen in quite some time. It was the way my mother used to grin whenever I did something cute or new.

Looking back now, I can see that Ritchie took me under his wing in a way. At meal times, he'd scoop food onto a plate and then hold it out to me before the others emptied the bowls. I noticed how, sometimes, he'd slow down when walking ahead of me if Patty or Norman came the other way, stepping out as if shielding me. I did notice the punches and slaps slowing down considerably whenever he was around. They still happened occasionally, but definitely not as often.

There was this one afternoon in particular when I found my new friend out behind our backyard sitting under a tree. This must have been about six or eight weeks after he'd arrived. Rather than the book I always saw in his hand, I saw a letter in one hand and a crumpled-up envelope in the other. I don't think he heard me approaching because when he saw me, he immediately turned away while wiping his face. There was no denying his crying, but of course, I didn't say anything. Ritchie wasn't too pleased that I saw him either.

"What the hell," he snapped while still facing the other way. "Don't you have anything better to do than sneak up on people?"

"I wasn't sneaking up," I said defensively before explaining my reason for being there. "Patty's drunk and beating on people. He already hit Ally hard enough to make her cry." When he didn't turn around to face me, I slowly backed away and went to head back to the hole in the fence to take my chances in the house. If I could make it back to my room, I'd found that hiding under the bed proved much more secure than just hiding under the blankets. Patty's knees didn't work so well, and the lower I hid, the better.

"Wait, kid," Ritchie called after me when I reached the hole in the fence and when I looked over my shoulder, he'd turned back to face me. "Maybe you can hang around for a bit." He waved me over, and feeling a grin straddle my face, I headed back to the log he was sitting on and dropped down beside him. It wasn't exactly comfortable, but anything was better than being near our supposed foster father.

"You're smart for getting out of there," he said after a few moments of silence. "Wouldn't want to be around if he ever loses complete control while drunk."

"Why, what would happen?"

Of course, I already knew the answer, but I liked listening to Ritchie explain things, and I think he enjoyed it as much as I did.

"I've seen guys like him before. Seen 'em put kids like you in the hospital. Broken arms, broken noses, stuff like that."

"He's mean," I said.

"Yeah, he is and I think he gets a real kick out of hurting people, so best to steer clear."

"He's only hit me a couple of times. I can usually dodge his fists quite easily."

"Yes, but you shouldn't have to," Ritchie said as he looked up into the sky, squinting to get a clear sight of a random cloud.

"But why would they let us stay with someone like that?"

It was a genuine question and one I'd thought about long before that day. I still had vivid flashbacks to when they came and dragged me out of my house, and I wondered why they would take me from a perfectly safe home to one like the Lightman's. Just as I knew he would, Ritchie had the answers.

"Because they need to show the courts that you're safe in a home."

"But we're *not* safe." He chuckled at that and gave me a pat on the back

"Yeah, but they don't care about that," Ritchie continued. "Not like anybody's gonna come and check up on things." He paused. "How did you get to be so smart, huh?"

"I dunno," I said, feeling my cheeks burn. "My mum was smart."

"Oh yeah? Where is she now?"

"They told me she's gone to heaven," I said and that's when another silence descended over us, this one a lot more uncomfortable.

I felt Ritchie tense up, the envelope in his left hand crunching as his fingers closed around it even tighter. I could see the knuckles turn white before one of them audibly popped. He didn't speak for a long time, and I honestly wasn't sure whether I had said the wrong thing. I was beginning to think that Heaven wasn't a place I was supposed to talk about. Anytime I did, people kind of got weird around me. And that was when he said the strangest thing to me, something that shook me at the time.

"Heaven isn't real, kid," was what he said before pushing himself off the log.

I watched him slowly walk towards the edge of the forest that sat behind our house. He didn't walk with purpose, more like slowly shuffling each of his feet in turn with no known destination. When I thought he might stop and come back, he only looked over his shoulder in my direction, maybe wondering if I was going to follow him. It didn't occur to me that he might have wanted me to, and maybe things would have played out very differently if I had.

Ritchie eventually crossed the threshold into the trees and after watching him for a few more minutes, I eventually lost track of him when the shadows swallowed him up. I remained on the log for what felt like forever, unsure of whether he'd come back for more talking or not. What I did find was my own mind wandering back to the last words he said to me, the idea that heaven not being real too hard for me to believe.

I think up until that moment, I'd still believed my mother might have come back for me at some point. Maybe she was trying to escape from whatever this heaven place was. Maybe she was being held against her will, and I was just staying in this place temporarily. I did hear some of the others talking about all the different homes they'd been to and figured that was where I would end up myself. The idea that heaven was just a made-up place created by people to try and make themselves feel better about death wasn't something I'd learn for at least another year.

When I eventually returned to the house, I did so only after standing by the hole in the fence, listening for any hint of Patty still shouting at anybody dumb enough to get close to him. The sun had dropped considerably by then, skirting the edge of the far horizon as a thick band of clouds followed close behind. By the time the rim of it began to disappear, those clouds hung directly overhead, threatening to drop their cargo of rainwater onto us.

The real moment of truth came when I heard Becky calling out her usual battle cry, announcing that dinner was ready. What followed sounded like an actual stampede as a dozen shoes galloped across the floorboards from the bedrooms to the kitchen. I was hungry, sure, but with no Ritchie to help me and the bulk of the kids already in the kitchen, I knew the chances of filling my belly that night were slim to none.

I did eventually go inside, of course, but my suspicions proved correct. All of the fish sticks were gone, and so was the majority of the potato mash. I did manage to scrape bits from the edges of the bowl and mix some of the remaining peas and carrots in to bulk it up. Filling it wasn't. A couple of the older kids stayed out in the living room to watch some television, a risk worth taking since Patty had fallen asleep on his side of the couch, and each shot me a sideways glance while taking nibbles from their fish sticks.

My bed had always proved my safe place, and that's where I took the dismal plate of food. I did take a quick look out the kitchen window to the hole in the fence on my way past but couldn't see any sign of Ritchie. My guess was he needed some time alone, something I totally understood even at my young and tender age.

The only word I could ever come up with to describe the food was bland. No matter which meal was served, it lacked the kind of taste I remembered from my mother's cooking. What everybody really longed for were the very occasional evenings when we might get treated to some takeaway. Fish and chips were my absolute favourite although I did only have it the one time when Patty won money at a card game the previous night. If you think the stampede was bad at regular meal times, you should have heard it when Becky called out for takeaway.

That night, I clearly remember taking my plate under the bed, lying on my stomach and resting my head on the side of my arm. The overhead light barely reached me under there, and I occasionally dipped my finger into the mash, using it like a makeshift fork. I was hungry, sure, but with limited food and my head full of confusing thoughts, actually eating it felt like an absolute chore.

I must have stayed under the bed for more than an hour as a couple of the others first took their plates back to the kitchen in the hope of finding something else and then returned to sit on their beds.

The conversation in the room didn't really change much from one day to the next, usually revolving around the latest movie or video game somebody needed to see or play. For me, it was those times when I used to close my eyes and pretend that those conversations were playing on some unseen screen, my own little movie playing right in front of me. To be honest, it was probably more so for me to feel like I was a part of their conversation, an actual participant whom they asked to join in.

The hardest thing for me during those first few months was the loneliness, something I can't begin to describe feeling as a six-year-old. How does a kid that young go from having a loving mother taking care of all his wants and needs to a kid completely unloved and unwanted? Crying myself to sleep on those cold and lonely nights only did so much to ease the pain. It was those moments hidden underneath the bed with eyes closed, pretending I was a part of their group, that I felt a sliver of what it meant to be wanted.

I went to bed that night feeling worse than ever. Maybe it was because of what Ritchie had told me, the idea that the reason for my mother's disappearance had been nothing but a lie. What if she abandoned me, and they were just too polite to tell me the truth? That was the other question I constantly asked myself. What if the love that she had shown me for as long as I could remember...what if that, too, was just a horrible lie?

The tears flowed a lot easier that night than most, and at one point, I forgot just where I was. When Norman rolled over in the bed above me, he hung his head over the edge of the bed and told me to shut the hell up. Two things immediately jumped into the forefront of my mind. The first was that I needed to control myself. The second was that Ritchie hadn't returned. If he had, there would have been no way that Norman would have spoken to me like that. He knew better, having witnessed the repercussions of doing so with Ritchie in the room first-hand.

Shut up, I did, almost immediately. Above me, I felt Norman roll back the other way and not long after, heard the slow and steady breathing as he fell asleep. I lay quietly alone in the dark, watching the light from the television out in the living room dance across the shadowy wall of the hallway. At some point, I did slip off, but little did I know the escape I yearned for most days would only be short-lived.

I don't know what came first, the bloodcurdling scream or the massive bang that sounded close enough to be in the room with us. The others sat up so fast. I could see their shadowy forms propped upright in the dark, but I didn't dare move. It was because of the TV lights still dancing across the wall that I knew it was still before midnight, the usual time that Becky would wake Patty up and head to bed. Sometimes, he'd follow her, and sometimes, she'd leave him there. There were also some nights where strange noises would come from their bedroom, the kind of noises that made some of the boys laugh, but those nights were rare.

We must have all figured it best not to move because nobody made an attempt to climb out of bed. The silence seemed to enclose each of us in our own bubbles as something shuffled out in the living room. I looked around the room at some of the shadows and could just make out faces, all turning to face each other as if expecting someone to have an answer.

To this day, I still don't know what compelled me to get out of bed, the youngest of the group with no possible chance to evade whatever horror was playing out in the next room. I heard someone whisper for me to get the hell back into bed, but I ignored them. There was something pulling me to the door, willing me to go forth and be the one who broke the moment.

When I reached the open doorway, I briefly looked to my left to where I could just make out Pete's face staring back at me. His was the only bed that benefited from the sliver of light falling into the room, and yet he still made sure to remain in the portion of his bed bathed in shadows. He hissed something at me, the terror in his tone more than evident, and while I wanted to stop there and then, my legs refused to listen to what my brain was telling them.

The first thing that struck me when I stepped into the hallway was the smell, the overwhelming scent of firecrackers in the air. At first, I wondered whether it was that night of the year when the skies lit up with bursts of colour, but then I remembered being inside. Fire-crackers were usually set off outside and usually in the company of grown-ups. Before my brain could make sense of the smell, something else mingled in, the subtle undertone somehow complementing the first smell.

Again, I wanted to stop, but something primal compelled me to continue on, an overwhelming sense of curiosity dragging me forth. A couple more steps further along, the scene before me opened enough to reveal three people in the room that so often held two. Becky sat in her usual spot on the couch nearest the back wall, her face contorted into a mass of horror. Patty sat in his recliner just as he always did, the backrest tilted back to allow the footrest up to support his hefty legs. Unfortunately, it wasn't his legs I was focusing on when I stopped in the middle of the doorway.

At first, I thought that Patty might have been sleeping. It was a common sight, and maybe it was because of that commonality that I couldn't make sense of the rest of what I was seeing. His head seemed to hang unnaturally to the right, his face pointing in my direction. The question running through my head was, why, if he was sleeping, were his eyes open? And if he wasn't sleeping, then why wasn't he up out of his seat, giving the final person in the room a good beating around the ears?

The answer should have come to me from the steady dripping of red fluid that continued pooling on the floor beside Patty's chair. The same fluid seemed to run across his face. I watched a thin stream of it flowing across his top lip, halfway down the cheek before dripping off in massive globules that splashed into the pool below like pebbles into a pond.

Ritchie hadn't moved since the moment he's shot Patty in the side of the head. While I didn't understand the entire moment until years later, I still remembered every microsecond of those few minutes, every bit of sensory perception stored and filed into the mind of a six-year-old kid. I don't how long exactly I stood there watching the scene from my spot but what I do know is that neither of them knew I was there until my stomach rumbled loudly with hunger.

It was Ritchie who spotted me first, looking around just enough to see what the noise had been. The revolver he still held straight out in front of him continued pointing at Patty, the barrel having barely moved since the shooting. I later wondered whether I could still see a tendril of blue smoke leaking out of the end of it, but I think that was just a kid's imagination adding some colour.

For a brief moment, the three of us just stared at each other in complete silence, the only one of us frozen with fear being Becky. She sat wide-eyed on the couch, her pupils bare pinpricks as she stared at the gun. I think she was so sure that Ritchie would turn the gun on her next that she resolved herself to her fate. Ritchie, however, had other ideas. Once he saw me standing in the doorway, he slowly began to lower the gun until it hung loosely by his side.

That would have been the perfect moment for Becky to move. If she had summoned enough courage, she might have even managed to disarm the much lighter kid standing in the middle of her living room. Even a kid my age knew that someone with three times the body mass could easily overpower someone so much lighter. Fear is what kept her on the couch and shock is what shackled her to it.

When Ritchie turned to see me standing there, at first, I thought he might have shot me as well. The look on his face is something I can truly never forget. It wasn't anger or rage or anything like that. Again, it took me years to fully recognize his expression, but I think he was relieved in a way, relieved to have finally freed himself from whatever troubles he'd carried.

"There ain't no heaven, kid," were the last words my first ever true friend said to me. The words were still hanging in the air a few seconds after he calmly raised the gun, pointed the barrel at his temple and pulled the trigger. I'll spare you the details of the specifics, but what I did notice was that for the first time in her life, Becky Lightman remained completely silent.

4

The true horror of what happened that night wasn't completely lost on a kid as young as me, a kid who would remember details of those events long after they slipped into the recesses of time. I don't know whether anybody else still remembers a skinny kid named Ritchie Blanton arriving at the home of Becky and Patty Lightman and immediately sending one of my first bullies onto his butt. It saddens me to think of his life ending the way it did, perhaps the biggest tragedy of all coming from the fact that he didn't get to live his life the way he wanted to.

If you think that Ritchie killing Patty Lightman improved our situation, I'm afraid you're mistaken. The system doesn't change just because you've seen a bit of tragedy. If anything, it kind of doubles down on its misery. In a way, Ritchie doing what he did sent the rest of us down a different path, one we might have tried to avoid if given the chance.

Less than four hours after the shooting, and about an hour after the first police officers began to leave the house, two minivans arrived in the dead of night. Each carried two people, who immediately told us to grab our belongings and climb into one of the vans. I didn't know it at the time, but it actually mattered which you chose because both vans went to very different places.

There wasn't much for me to grab, just a tiny bag made up mostly of clothes that I could have left there without feeling a loss. Tired, hungry, and with a kind of numbness clinging to me, I climbed into the first van I came to, grabbed a seat near the middle and closed my eyes. I didn't care who was already sitting on it nor who followed me aboard. All I wanted was to sleep, with the hope of waking up and finding that it had all been nothing more than a vivid nightmare. If fate answered my call, I'd open my eyes and find myself back in my old bed, my mum out in the kitchen smoking a cigarette while watching some random program on the small TV. Sadly, it wasn't to be.

The drive only lasted about twenty minutes, and when one of the people eventually opened the sliding door and told us to get out, I noticed that the second van hadn't followed us.

"Where are the others," someone behind me asked, but answers weren't something given freely in our world.

"Just get inside," the woman said with less than a friendly tone and feeling like prisoners arriving at jail, we walked into a place I would very quickly come to hate even more than the Lightman's home.

The Thames Home for Boys wasn't what those assigned to the place called it. Whispering Hall was what the residents knew it as, and for very good reason. Rather than individual rooms, all of the beds had been set up in three neat rows of five double bunks, thirty kids of varying ages made to live inside what might have been a church at some point. Given the openness of the place and the distinct lack of heating for those caught inside, you could imagine how miserable the existence must have been.

If I thought privacy was an issue at the Lightman's, then I was about to be given a rude awakening. Not only did I now sleep amongst a group of thirty, but we also had to share a single bathroom containing just two cubicles. This wasn't a place where you could find a quiet corner to hide. In fact, there wasn't anywhere in the place a person could go to be alone, especially from those intent on heaving more misery on those weaker than them.

While Norman Green might have been my first bully, he was by no means my last. I wasn't the youngest at Whispering Hall, but the two that were younger also happened to have already formed alliances long before my arrival, and that meant I was again the weakest of all. Barely a minute after waking up that first morning, a kid named Brian Dunn walked to my bed, ripped the pillow out from under my head and told me to curl up my jacket or something. When I went to say something back, he held up a fist and waited for me to speak. The silence of those watching on told me more than words ever could. I could either learn fast or hurt fast.

What little dignity I had left vanished over the next few weeks as my existence went from bad to worse. If the kids weren't enough to contend with, the priests running the place were even worse. While I had the benefit of being able to leave the Lightman's home for school several times a week, the same thing couldn't be said for Whispering Hall. Built right next to one of the strictest Catholic schools in the country, I managed to walk out of one miserable situation into another when attending classes each day.

While the teachers certainly didn't help our miserable existence, it was the other kids who reigned terror on those whom they called The Rag Brigade, those unfortunate enough to call the place next door home. It wasn't difficult to spot us, I guess. Our clothes alone were an easy giveaway, most of them already worn well past their prime and usually either a size or two either too small or too big. All a kid had to do was stand back and take one look at us, and it was obvious where we came from.

And it wasn't just our clothes. Given the bathroom situation, most of us younger kids hated the thought of going in there to wash up, while those older than us couldn't be bothered at all. It wasn't as if anybody really cared, and with nobody to make sure our hygiene was up to standard, the cleanliness just kind of flew out of the window.

The Rag Brigade was a name I came to despise more than the place itself. Life was already bad enough, but to then have those more fortunate than us actually try to add yet more misery by pointing out our flaws...it just felt like hell. I don't think I ever felt quite like human rubbish the way I did those first few weeks at Whispering Hall. What I hoped for the most was to grow faster than humanly possible so I'd be able to defend myself against such hate.

It's funny looking back at those days during the first year at the place, the things you remember and those you try your hardest to forget. What I remember the most is the feeling of relief when the lights finally went out in the hall each night. It was Father Callahan who made his final round of the evening and the one who ultimately switched the overhead lights off when he finished.

"Sleep well, lads," was how he always ended the moment before closing the door and leaving us alone for the night. The rattle of the key as he locked us in kind of echoed the feeling of complete hopelessness.

At first, there would always be silence for a couple of minutes as people made sure we were really alone. Then somebody would whisper something, a few others would giggle, and then those lucky enough to have smuggled in torches would light them up. What followed would be a couple of hours of chaos, but the kind of chaos that barely sounded louder than a whisper.

Sometimes, a pack of boys would choose a victim and torment them relentlessly, stealing their bedding, maybe beating them, or doing whatever they could do to get a reaction. Other times, they might just congregate around someone's bed and just talk, whisper about the latest movie or video game, or whatever girl they fancied at the time.

For me, most of those nights, I would lie curled up under my blanket and try to dream myself out of the place. Sleep became my most fantastic escape, a friend to embrace, and it was there that I could live whatever dreams that great abyss allowed me to. It was also how I managed to survive through almost an entire year in the place, Whispering Hall, becoming one continuous nightmare with my only reprieve being those nights. That was until the night I found myself at the very centre of one of their tormenting sessions.

Each night, when the lights were switched off, I always waited for the snickering to start to try and figure out where their attention was aimed. You usually had a fair idea based on the mood before bedtime. If somebody had an issue with someone, it became pretty obvious, especially if it involved one of the lads from the main group. Then you knew there would be a targeted pack attack.

Unfortunately, you also knew when their attention was on you because of any number of signs you'd see ahead of time. One night in particular, about three months after my seventh birthday, I happened to get in the way of one of the worst bullies at Whispering Hall, this considerable kid called Brandon something or other. I don't remember his last name as it was something foreign that seemed to contain endless amounts of letters. I don't think it makes any difference to the story. The point is, I tripped him up quite by accident, sending him tumbling to the floor as the plate of food he'd been holding smashed before him.

The rest of the dining room immediately went silent as Brandon first sat up and then rose to his feet, the process taking more than a little effort, given his size. By the time he rounded on me, his face had turned a bright shade of crimson that reached all the way to his ears. Before he had a chance to grab my shirt and shake the crap out of me, Father Callahan came into the room to see what the noise had been about. Thankfully, he arrived right before Brandon could take a swing at me.

If that had been the end of it, things might have turned out a little better, but unfortunately for both Brandon and me, the second the kid went to grab himself a new plate of food, Father Callahan called for him to clean up the mess.

"If you're not hungry enough to hold onto your first plate, boyo, I'm not about to let you waste another," he said as he gestured for Brandon to follow him. The look I got as he walked past me was enough to tell me that this wasn't over.

When Brandon returned a few minutes later, carrying a mop and bucket, he looked ready to bodyslam anybody who got in his way. I swear I could have pictured angry thunderheads circling around his head, the anger radiating off him. Nobody dared make a sound while he cleaned the spilt food, and while I didn't look directly at him, I could feel his gaze in my direction every so often. Some of the others did likewise, and I think they all knew that I was practically a dead kid waiting for fate.

I'll never forget the walk back to the hall after that meal, one of the longest walks of my life. The heaviness in my stomach stretched deep into the very centre of my soul, and the urge to use the toilet wasn't helping. If a hole had opened up before me with a bunch of rabid dogs waiting for me at the bottom, I would have gladly taken my chances and jumped in. I knew I had it coming. The only question was what *it* would actually be. How far would Brandon go to take his humiliation out on me?

As it turned out, it was a lot worse than I expected. Remember, I was just a seven-year-old kid, barely old enough to understand the reason for us being there in the first place. I'd heard them dish out their pain plenty of times but never expected it to be me on the receiving end. Oh, how I begged the universe to keep the lights on just a little longer to delay whatever punishment I had coming my way. Unfortunately for me, fate had other ideas.

Just as he always did, Father Callahan walked his final rounds at precisely nine o'clock, and just as usual, he gave us his last message for the night.

"Sleep well, lads," were what I expected to be the final words I'd ever hear before my miserable existence came to an end. The snap of the light switch sounded more like a gunshot as it echoed across the room, and my heart immediately took off. The shadows I had longingly craved for so long suddenly felt like enemy territory, descending over me with nothing but betrayal waiting for me within.

For those first few seconds, my senses, those I needed to focus on the most, peaked in a way I had never experienced before. I swear I could have heard a pin drop, my hearing almost a superpower while my eyes desperately tried to adjust to the darkness. The silence sounded overwhelmingly hostile, a threatening veil of abuse hanging over my bed. For those first few seconds, I held my breath in anticipation of what was to come next, expecting the shuffling to begin at any moment. Once it did, it would signal the others to also start making their move, and I would quickly find myself surrounded by those ready to do me harm.

Time seemed to slow down to just a crawl, the seconds dwindling by a fraction at a time. I think I must have held my breath for way too long, the pressure in my chest building the more I focused on other parts of my body. When the attack did finally come, just as I knew it would, it did so from an entirely different direction.

A hand suddenly grabbed me from the top of my head, the fingers snatching a handful of hair before dragging me out from the bed across the railing behind me. I thought my scalp was going to rip off entirely; such was the excruciating pain radiating down through my face.

"Don't make a sound, weazel," Brandon hissed into my ear, the smell of stale spit almost making me gag.

He beat me. Brandon used me as a punching bag for God knows how long, as the rest of those in the hall lay silently in their beds, listening. I can't begin to tell you how painful those few minutes were as his fists and feet laid into me like a regular brawler. I had to lock my jaw closed to keep from calling out and felt warmth run down my face from several points as he opened me up.

That was the first proper beating of my life, but by no means the last. It left me battered and bruised in a way I didn't think possible, the pain beyond anything I had ever endured. Some of the injuries I wouldn't see until morning, and even then, a kind of numbness shielded me from the absolute agony.

What I want to tell you is that when the door finally unlocked again, and Father O'Brien made his morning rounds, he spotted my injuries and immediately ushered me down to the office for some medical attention. A bandaid or two for my cuts and a warm washcloth with which to wipe the blood from my face. Perhaps a friendly word about how he would make sure that this type of treatment would never be unleashed on me again. I *wish* that's what I could tell you.

"What in the name of the Lord have you done to your sheet, lad," was what he *did* say when he walked past my bed.

I'd unknowingly used the top of the sheet as a kind of cloth and wiped some of the blood from my face. It stained the piece of bedding bad enough for him to notice. When I raised my head, his eyes grew wider as he spotted more blood on my pillow. Climbing out of bed, I did manage a quick look across to where Brandon was sitting on the edge of his bed, and the grin on his face spoke volumes.

I lost my television rights for a week, and I also had my desserts cancelled. To a kid with nothing positive in his life, it felt like the final piece of my heart had been torn free and nailed to a wall. They might as well have. With not much left to live for, there seemed just a single option left for me to take and for a kid as young as me, it was an option I failed to completely understand.

5

Given the layout of both Whispering Hall itself and the strict regime the priests kept us under, my plan wasn't one easily set in motion. All I knew was that I needed to get away from the place, no matter the method. I figured running away might open up a new life for me and lead me down a path of undiscovered opportunities. To be honest, all manner of crazy thoughts and wild visions filled my head the day before I actually made the idea a reality. I even believed I might actually find a circus somewhere on my travels, and I'd be adopted and taken on the road.

The problem was that neither the school nor Whispering Hall left much room open for escape. If they did, I suspect that most kids calling the place home would have already shot through, and since nobody had, it was obvious the chance for escape was virtually impossible. And yet, I had to try. With my body battered and bruised almost as much as the sensitive soul inside, I knew I had to give it a go, even if just to save myself for a day or two.

Once I made the decision to actually go through with it, I began to carefully pay attention to the little things throughout my day, the moments where escape might be a slim chance. The walk between Whispering Hall and school, the playground during lunch break, and perhaps slipping out through the windows after lights out. I began to quietly watch from afar, memorizing each and every moment throughout the day, spying on the routes and actions of the teachers, the routines of the priest, and most importantly, the awareness of my fellow captives.

In the end, it took me just a couple of days to find the opportunity I'd been searching for, the eventual solution probably one of the simplest of all. At the end of each day, a few moments after the final bell rang for the school day's conclusion, the hallway bore the brunt of bustling children let out of class, each keen to get home and undertake whatever awesome activity they had planned. Those heading back to Whispering Hall would fight their way through the crowd, clawing against the current to reach the top of the corridor where the door led out into the yard closest to *our* home.

Standing at both ends of the hall were the priests allocated to supervise the end-of-day rush and no doubt ensure that each kid went in the direction they were supposed to. All I had to do was keep my head low enough when passing by to make sure my face wasn't noticed. I couldn't do much about my clothes, of course, or the mop of hair way overdue for a haircut, but if I managed to stick close to the back of a taller kid, who knew how my stealthy plan would play out?

I honestly don't know whether I was more nervous waiting for Brandon to come and beat the shit out of me that night or waiting for the bell that afternoon. I must have sat staring at the clock hanging above the whiteboard nonstop for the last part of the day, intently watching the second hand work its way around the face no less than a couple of dozen times. Each time it reached the top again, I saw it as another minute closer to my final escape.

When the bell did eventually ring, I made sure to hang back and not be one of the first out through the door. What I needed was cover, and without plenty of other people already around me, my chances of getting through were slim. The other thing I needed was to avoid those heading back to Whispering Hall. If any of them saw me, I didn't think they'd keep their mouths shut.

Looking back now, I honestly don't know how I managed to get away with it, but the escape proved to be far easier than I ever anticipated. The two gatekeepers I had to slip past were both distracted by other students, giving me just enough time to rush past, along with countless others. Once out on the street, I mostly remained close behind a group of about eight who continued on towards the next intersection, passing by cars holding parents waiting patiently for their children. Nobody seemed to show me the slightest interest.

Two blocks down, I peeled off from my chosen group by ducking down a side alley. I began running almost immediately, the pounding in my chest reaching a fever pitch as a mix of adrenaline and fear fueled my legs onward. At the end of the lane, I crossed another street, re-entered the lane on the other side, and continued until I eventually reached the final mouth, where train tracks ran next to the adjoining street. Once I crossed the street, I climbed through a hole in the chain-link fence, looked left and right for options and followed a small dirt track into the brush.

The further I ran, the more I was sure I would finally find something that would keep me from returning to my previous nightmare, a kind stranger to take me in, or even that proverbial circus I'd been told so much about. It wasn't long before I slowed down due to the dry uncomfortableness in my throat, a thirst unlike anything I'd ever felt before. Beads of sweat had begun running down the sides of my face, and that was the first moment when I suddenly realized the complexity of the situation.

I had never run away from anywhere before, much less a place that had, up until that moment, provided me with all the things I needed to survive. Food, drink, a place to sleep. It had never occurred to me prior to that moment that I could take none of those things with me. Now, out in the real world, it was up to me to find suitable replacements, and I suddenly realized that I hadn't had the life experience to know how.

"Hey, kid, someone chasing you?"

Without realizing it, I'd stopped running and paused next to an abandoned house that backed onto the tracks. Guess my sudden realization caused my legs to stop working. I looked over to where a couple of men sat around a small fire they'd lit in some sort of rusty container, both looking in my direction.

For a second, we just stared back at each other from opposing ends, one of the men holding a cigarette in front of his mouth as if time had stopped. I felt an uneasiness wash over me, a new kind of panic seeping in that took me a moment to recognize.

"Come and grab some warmth over here," the first man said and began waving me over.

That was when my legs suddenly came to life again and began propelling me down the track at twice the previous speed. Driven by instinct, something took hold of me, willing me to get the hell out of there. I still don't know to this day whether those guys were as bad as my immature brain believed, but instinct is a powerful thing. Who knows how things might have played out if I'd hung around?

I don't know for how long I continued running, but what I do remember is that when I eventually stopped, my lungs felt on fire as my heart threatened to beat right out of my chest. Collapsing to the ground in a heap of exhaustion, I could barely get enough air into me, desperately sucking in large mouthfuls while lying on my back on some grassy patch beneath a tree. The place looked about as isolated as any I'd already passed, and with a few hundred meters since I ran by the last house, I figured it as good a spot as any to take a breather.

Staring up at the sky, I tried to focus on the shape of the clouds to take my mind off the furious beating inside me. I had never passed out from exhaustion before, and feeling a strange dizziness overwhelm me caused my already angry heart to pick up the pace. And how does a confused, frightened, and highly emotional kid get himself through such a terrifying moment? With laughter, of course.

I began to laugh the moment I thought I spotted a pig's face staring back at me from the sky, this oddly shaped cloud hanging directly above me. It appeared more as an actual pig as opposed to some weird cartoonish character, and it was the sight of it that sent me into hysterics. For a brief moment in time, I didn't care about who might hear me or who might have been watching from behind the vegetation surrounding me. All I knew was that the pig reminded me of Father Callahan in a way, the ample jowl eerily similar between the two.

The laughing must have continued for at least ten minutes, by which time my exhaustion had multiplied. With the ringlet of trees and bushes shielding me from the chilly wind, it wasn't long before the warmth of the sunshine sent me drifting off into sleep. I was, after all, a kid in limbo, one with no destination to head to or time frame to be there. I was a tumbleweed in the wind, temporarily snagged to a comfortable bed of grass and soft sand.

The problem with being seven was that I had virtually zero experience with perception, and what felt like a dream come true during the daylight hours quickly turned into a full-blown nightmare when I woke to find myself caught up in a world of shadows. When I first woke, I sat up so violently that I felt something bite into my back, a muscle giving out under strain. With eyes wide, I looked around wildly, trying to work out where the hell I was, and it took me a moment to remember the events leading me to where I now sat.

A thick layer of cloud had blown in from the other side of the city at some point, and with no moon beyond them, the darkness hung a lot heavier over my neck of the world. The sheer weight of the shadows consumed any hint of light, giving me virtually no chance to make out any of the features of my hideout. You couldn't really call it a hideout since it had no real structure to it, but it's what I remember feeling it to be.

That wasn't the first time my senses had been piqued in terror, but unlike those nights in either Whispering Hall or the Lightman home, this was the first time where I truly was on my own. My hearing took on an almost superpower-like ability, able to detect the faintest of noises travelling vast distances. I listened to countless dogs barking, unseen cars impatiently blowing their horns, and somewhere behind me, someone yelled something unintelligible into the air.

Closer to me, I heard some unseen animal scurry through the underbrush while a distance ahead, an owl or other kind of bird began hoo-hooing into the night. When a distinctive crack of a twig snapping beneath someone's foot broke close to where I was standing, my insides tightened in an instant grip of fear. I spun around to try and see the source of the noise, expecting to find some hooded, knife-wielding figure closing in on me, but the shadows again opted to betray me. The darkness felt as if it was about to consume me.

Frozen with fear, I held my breath, doing everything possible to silence whatever noise I was making. My eyes felt like homing lasers, desperate to lock onto whatever had begun stalking me in the night as they scoured every inch of the hidden landscape before me. A train's whistle suddenly ripped across the night sky, quickly followed by a familiar rattling of dead weight rolling across the tracks. High-pitched screeching occasionally pierced the air, but all I could do was continue searching for demons.

When a voice suddenly spoke to me moments after the noise of the train died down again, the panic took hold of me in a way I'd never felt before. My legs took off long before the rest of me did, and for a split second, I thought I was going to screw up the simplicity of running and end up sprawled on the ground, but it was my agility that kept the rest of me in check.

Running through the night in whatever direction my legs carried me, it felt like every monster in hell had been unleashed onto me. I must have sprinted for God knows how long, praying that my feet wouldn't tangle themselves up or catch on a rogue tree root or other unseen obstacle. I don't know whether it was the fear itself or just the over-imaginative mind of a kid, but I swear I could feel hot breath on the back of my neck, each step bringing whatever had begun chasing me closer. Death felt closer than ever as I spotted the same fire I'd passed by hours earlier, the two faces of those previous men staring out at the shadow running past. I could have stopped and asked for help, but fear drove me on.

The laneways that followed passed by in a blur as I continued on, running as fast as my little legs could carry me. My eyes continuously scanned for any upcoming threats, but I think by then, any hint of movement, no matter how insignificant, would have panicked me further. It wasn't until I finally emerged onto a road lit up by street-lights that I finally eased off the accelerator pedal enough to take inventory of my new location.

Talk about fear. Despite the cold, my shirt felt drenched with sweat, and the slight breeze hitting me felt like ice as it blew across my dripping face. I began shivering before my breathing had a chance to return to normal, and feeling a lot more exposed out in the open, I started looking for somewhere new to hide. A suburban street was the last place I expected to find myself, but now that I was there, it did feel a lot safer than some isolated track out in the middle of nowhere.

Each of the homes lining the street looked blacked out, and it didn't occur to me that it must have already been well after midnight. Who knew how long I lay passed out within my tiny circle of underbrush and trees before running wildly into the night like a deranged lunatic? Headlights suddenly lit up my section of the foot-path, and I shrunk back into an open gateway as a taxi suddenly passed by. I could just make out the driver's face behind the steering wheel, lit up by the instrument panel. I was so sure that he would turn and see me standing there that I dropped to my knees just to avoid detection.

I didn't stand again until the sound of the engine entirely disappeared again, and once it did, I looked around the small front yard for any possible hiding place. The thin strip of flowerbed running along the inside perimeter didn't exactly offer me anything significant, but there was a bush in the corner closest to the home that looked substantial enough. I walked a little closer as the shivering intensified, found the grass beneath the bush soft enough to use as a bed and dropped down behind the clump of vegetation.

For those first few minutes, I just lay there shaking uncontrollably, my fingers pushing deep into the bottom of my pockets, where my body warmth would keep them from freezing. I had never felt more alone than I did at that moment. The fear of not knowing how I would go on once the sun came up, the cold biting into every part of my body, and the hunger continuing to build inside me. My situation felt utterly hopeless, and yet I knew that I couldn't go back to Whispering Hall.

The floodgates truly opened once the first couple of tears began to fall, and I found myself sobbing uncontrollably. Squeezing my eyes shut as tight as possible, I tried to keep the tears falling to a minimum, but it was no good. There were just some things a soul needed to shed. It was while squeezing my eyes shut that a voice suddenly whispered to me, but while it did scare the absolute crap out of me, I could tell right away that there was no threat behind it.

"Are you alright, dear?"

I opened my eyes to see a face staring down at me, the older woman kneeling down at the edge of the garden bed. She looked to have a dressing gown wrapped around herself, pulling one side of it tight as she used the other hand for balance.

"Why don't you come inside? You must be freezing."

"I'm lost," was all I could manage, the lie slipping out a lot easier than expected. Actually, I didn't think it was quite as deceitful as it might have sounded since I was, in fact, lost, both physically and mentally. The woman pointed to somewhere above me.

"I like to sleep with my window open just a bitsy, and I heard you rustling around out here. Why don't we get you inside before we wake Mr. Hampstead up?"

She held out a hand to me, and something about the way she smiled pushed the rest of my apprehension away. A kind of relief washed over me as I felt the warmth of her skin on mine while she grabbed my hand and half-pulled me off the ground. She looked out onto the street as another car passed by and ushered me inside.

Once she closed the door, the woman led me into her kitchen, where she immediately stoked the fire inside an old stove and waved me over.

"Come and grab some of this heat," she said with a warm smile, and I sat on a chair that she pulled closer. "Now, how about a nice cup of hot chocolate?"

I nodded enthusiastically and watched as she proceeded to grab a bottle of milk from the fridge.

"I'm Elizabeth, and what might your name be, young man?"

"Jack Hardy."

"I'm pleased to meet you, Jack Hardy," she said, again offering me that warm smile as she scooped some cocoa into the saucepan she had sitting on the stove.

When she handed me the cup a few minutes later, what I tasted was more than just a gooey warmth of happiness. For a brief moment, what I felt in those mouthfuls of sweetness was freedom, the kind I could barely remember ever experiencing before that moment. I wanted to hang onto that moment for as long as possible, each mouthful smaller than the previous, in the hope of stretching the hot chocolate out as far as possible.

Unfortunately, Elizabeth Hampstead didn't end up becoming my saviour the way I had hoped. Not long after finishing my drink, a weary-looking old man walked out into the kitchen, greeted me with one eye closed and confusingly gestured to his wife. Twenty minutes later, the knock on the door signalled not only the end of my time with the first friendly face I'd met in a long time but also my overall freedom. The police who showed up wasted little time in getting some answers out of me, and before the sun rose up that very same morning, those same police officers handed me back to the priests of Whispering Hall. I had been returned right back to the very nightmare I'd been trying to escape.

6

That might have been the very first escape I managed to go through with, but it was by no means the last. The thing I still remember, even while sitting here writing this after all these years, is the sweetness of that first mouthful of hot chocolate. That first hint of bitter essence cutting through the sweetness, the melted silky smoothness of pure joy tingling every nerve ending in my mouth. Sometimes, I can close my eyes and feel the same goosebumps breaking out across my body, re-tasting that moment in vivid detail.

While the priests tried their hardest to stop me, I began to break out regularly, sometimes staying out for a couple of days at a time. At one point, I tried to retrace my steps to Elizabeth Hampstead's in the hopes of getting just one more taste of that hot chocolate, but I never found her home again. It somehow vanished into the same spirals of time where my mother continues to dwell, a hidden world only visible inside my mind.

Days turned into weeks and weeks into months, and before I knew it, all the little moments that made life what it is began to pass me by. My eighth birthday gave way to my ninth, my ninth to my tenth, and with each passing year, I continued struggling through a life I felt powerless to escape from. The faces inside Whispering Hall occasionally changed, with some kids leaving while others arrived. The old ones welcomed the new ones with the same abrasive greeting that I faced upon my own arrival, quickly being shown the unwritten rules we lived by. Occasionally, previous kids would return, welcomed back into the ranks by their peers with open arms.

If you haven't yet guessed, it was the dream of every kid living at Whispering Hall to be selected by an adopting family and finally saved from a life of torturous hell. We'd see their cars pull up out the front of the place, eager couples climbing out and being met by one of the attending social workers with whom they had been dealing. You could feel the energy in the room, every kid's senses immediately turning their detectors in the direction of the visitors in the hope of finally having their card pulled.

I watched multiple families come and go over the months and years, each taking their chosen child with them in the hope of building whatever family dream they'd imagined for themselves. Each time someone I knew got to pack their bags, they'd always leave wearing this grin that spoke volumes. Sometimes, it was the sort of grin you wanted to slap right off their face but knew you couldn't.

There came a point in my life where I figured it would never be me who got to walk out of Whispering Hall in the company of a new family. I'd resolved myself to the fact that I didn't have the kind of *look* prospective parents were looking for, something about my appearance just not the right fit. What made it even harder was the fact I couldn't tell the difference between my look and everyone else living in the place, which was why I believed the reason for my continuous rejection to be something running a lot deeper. That was until the afternoon of Sunday, February 9, 1997. I was eleven years old, and my life was about to change.

I often wondered whether fate would somehow give advance warning of an incoming significant change, but I can honestly say that when I woke up that Sunday morning, I didn't feel any different. The weather outside looked just as miserable as always, a light rain continuing to turn the wintery blanket of dirty snow into a righteous sludge fest. The sun had been missing in action for going on a week, and the boredom of having to remain indoors was beginning to bite hard.

It was just after lunch that someone called out that a fresh boatload of prospective families had pulled up out the front of the building. Some of the kids ran over to get a good look at them, but truth be told, I couldn't be bothered. I'd managed to sneak an old Ritchie Rich comic into my bed, one that I had found discarded in the school playground a few days earlier. I'd already read it multiple times, but given the outside weather conditions and kids lined up three deep to use the gaming system, the options to combat my boredom were extremely limited.

The procedure for the incoming families was always the same, with one of the priests usually meeting said parents and their assigned social worker in the main office. They'd spend a few minutes going over whatever paperwork still needed to be sorted, and then they'd send one of the duty helpers to come and fetch the lucky chosen. The assigned helpers were normally one of the older kids who worked for certain privileges, a duty that was highly sought after.

Imagine my surprise when the name called out that afternoon was mine, a name I never expected to hear in a million years. I don't think anybody else had either because the immediate silence that fell across the room felt more like shock than surprise.

"Jack, let's go," Colin called out a second time. "Let's not keep them waiting."

What followed were ten of the most extraordinary minutes of my life as I felt them pass by as something akin to a movie. It didn't feel as if I was inside my own body at all, somehow watching the scene unfold on some invisible television screen. After packing my things and wishing those watching on goodbye, Colin led me out of the hall, along the first corridor, and down the stairs. Waiting for me at the bottom was Father Callahan, the social worker named Alison Farrow, and two people I didn't recognize. Judging by the warmth of their smiles and that unsure look of expectation, I guessed them to be my new parents.

"Jack, I'd like you to meet Mr. And Mrs. French," Father Callahan said when I stopped on the second to last step.

"Brian and Wendy, please," the woman said, her smile growing wide enough to show teeth.

"I'm Jack," I said and shook with each of them after they held their hands out to me.

The transition from Whispering Hall ward of the state to a newly adopted kid heading home happened in the blink of an eye. One moment, I'm standing in the foyer, listening to others talking about me as if I wasn't standing right there beside them, the next, I'm climbing into the back seat of a Range Rover, ready to start a new life. It's incredible just how fast fate will work when it really wants to.

From the moment the doors of the car closed, and Brian pulled out into traffic, Wendy began asking me all sorts of questions, the kind someone asked when trying to make small talk. I could tell she felt uncomfortable, unlike her husband, who just stole the occasional glance at me in the rearview mirror. I'd thought about this day a lot during my time at Whispering Hall, the moment when a family would finally take a chance on me. It definitely didn't play out how I had imagined it would, the actual experience a far cry from what I had anticipated.

The transition from orphan to new family member happened in the blink of an eye and was definitely not the amazing fanfare I often daydreamed about. It felt flat, lacking the kind of jubilation I imagined myself to feel. If anything, the nerves kind of ruined the moment for me. There was no celebration, no fists pumped into the air. I simply grabbed my things, shook my new parents' hands and climbed into their car before finding myself whisked towards a new existence waiting for me somewhere north of the city.

Along the way to my new home, Wendy kept telling me all about the wonderful places I could explore in the surrounding area. According to her, Enfield boasted a large number of parks where kids my age often played football and cricket, threw frisbees, or just hung out with friends. I wasn't much of a sporty kind of person, but I didn't have the heart to tell her so. Instead, I just nodded occasionally to acknowledge her words before turning my gaze out of the window again.

While I knew the opportunity was huge, it might sound strange to you to learn that I actually questioned whether moving in with a new family was the right move for me. Don't get me wrong, I know just how lucky I was. I don't want to sound ungrateful but the truth is, I had kind of gotten used to life at Whispering Hall. Yes, it wasn't the best, not by a long way, but it was a life I understood, and since I hadn't died in the years I'd lived there, perhaps it wasn't so bad after all.

Who are you kidding? I remember mouthing to myself when the thought popped into my head. Why the hell *wouldn't* I be happy at the prospect of living in a typical house again? Real food, perhaps my own room, the chance to go to a normal school and not be seen as one of the Rag Brigade. I think I felt my cheeks heat up with embarrassment at not seeing this as an incredible opportunity.

An hour after walking out of Whispering Hall for what I eventually hoped would be for the last time, Brian and Wendy welcomed me into their home with open arms. They first showed me to my new room, which could have been taken right out of my dreams. A timber bed with a Teenage Mutant Ninja Turtle bedspread. On the white walls hung a couple of posters of cars, one a bright red Ferrari, the other a Yellow Lamborghini. The window was huge, overlooking a backyard that backed onto one of the parks Wendy had told me about, the green landscape stretching off into the distant woods. And that's when I saw him.

"You have a dog?"

"We do," Brian said with a grin. "His name is Peanut. Want to come downstairs and meet him?"

I could barely contain my excitement as I followed my new parents back down to the ground floor and out into the backyard. A little bundle of fur began to circle my feet at a great rate of knots, the Pug excitedly barking as it bounded from one side of me to the other.

"Hey, boy," I kept saying as I tried to pat the little guy and when he finally slowed enough for me to scratch him behind the ear, I dropped to the ground. Peanut began jumping up against me, his tongue lapping at my cheeks and nose, desperate to let me know his excitement. I don't think I ever laughed harder, the moment one I could barely comprehend.

"You'll also meet Vicky later this afternoon," Wendy said once I managed to stem the tongue attack enough to hear her.

"Vicky?"

"Yes, she visits her mum every second weekend." The idea of living with a girl hadn't crossed my mind before, and I did find it somewhat intriguing.

Not only did I get to live with a family who had their very own dog, but I also gained a new sister, so to speak. I knew she wasn't technically my *real* sister, but under the circumstances, I wasn't about to argue about specifics. I guessed that was how adopted families operated, each person willing to accept certain aspects of the situation while overlooking others. If I were going to pretend I was part of a new family, then I would need to accept all of it, even calling a complete stranger my sister.

When Vicky walked into the house a few hours later, I didn't think she was completely happy to see me. Not only did she completely avoid any eye contact with me, but I don't think she even heard Wendy introduce me to her. She did shake my hand, but there was very little commitment behind the exchange, her grip barely detectable. She wore her long black hair pulled back into a ponytail, exposing her stern face in a way that might have intimidated some.

"Give her time," Wendy whispered to me once Vicky left the room and headed upstairs. "She's had a rough weekend. She normally does when she visits her mother." It was the tone in Wendy's voice that told me she didn't approve of Vicky's mother; something was definitely amiss.

Vicky didn't join us for dinner that night, despite Wendy assuring me that she would. We ended up having pizza, and I got to choose my very own, something I had never experienced before. Imagine a kid eleven years old and getting excited at the prospect of getting to order his very own pizza for the first time. That kind of sums up the type of existence I'd led up until that moment.

That night, I thought I would sleep better than I had ever slept before, but it might surprise you to learn that I did anything but. In fact, it might have possibly been one of the worst nights of my life, ranking even further down than my very first night at Whispering Hall. Why, I hear you ask? Fear.

Every time I found myself drifting off, I'd wake up seconds later with a start, believing the entire day to have been nothing more than a dream I didn't want to wake up from. The idea that I didn't deserve to be where I was hadn't yet taken complete hold, but I was well on the way to believing it. Questions began to arise, haunting me every time I dared close my eyes. What if fate had made a mistake? What if it wasn't me they had come to collect but someone else entirely, and I was simply a clerical error? What if I woke up the next morning and Father Callahan was waiting for me by the front door, ready to drag me back to where I really belonged?

I lay in my new bed, watching the shadows of the outside tree dancing across my walls for almost the entire night. I'm not sure at which point I did finally drop off, but when I woke again, the shadows had disappeared, replaced by the bright rays of sunshine streaming in through the window. The veil of brain fog I normally woke up with had somehow failed to follow me to the new house, and when I jumped out of bed, I did so with the kind of energy and enthusiasm I hadn't felt in a very long time. It was the sheer exhilaration of realizing that it hadn't been a dream after all, and this was the beginning of a life I had always longed for. What I didn't know was that by the end of the following day, all sense of security would be gone, replaced by something completely unexpected.

7

That first official day waking up in the Frenchs' home, now my home, was unlike anything I had ever experienced before, not even living with my own mother, from what I remember. Coming downstairs and being first greeted by the rich smell of frying bacon and freshly baked bread, then by my new foster mother, gave me a real sense of want, if that makes sense. Despite being there, living in the moment, I just wanted it to feel even stronger, to somehow convince me that it wasn't just an illusion. I wanted the ticket of admission tattooed on my arm, if that makes sense.

"How did you sleep, sport?" Brian asked as I sat down at the table, taking up my newly appointed position.

"Great," I said, then immediately felt bad for telling my first lie.

"Wasn't sure what you like to eat for breakfast," Wendy said as she pointed to a couple of boxes of still-sealed cereal, as well as a basket of fresh apples and bananas. "I'm making Brian his usual bacon and eggs if you'd like some of those as well."

"I'll go the Froot Loops if that's OK," I said, secretly yearning to find out what those sweet ringlets of supposed *real fruit* actually tasted like, having never had them before.

"Froot Loops, it is," Wendy said and handed me a bowl before pushing the chosen box closer to me. "Help yourself."

That first taste sent shivers down my spine, the second, goose-bumps along my arms. I was swimming in a sea of childhood bliss when Vicky took her seat beside me, looking somewhat distracted.

"I got a new bottle of orange juice," Wendy said to her as she pulled it from the fridge. "Grab you a glass?"

"No, I'm fine," Vicky said, and I was surprised by the tone she used. It sounded almost dismissive, her eyes remaining on the apple she pulled from the fruit bowl.

"You sure, sweetie?"

"Yes, I have to get to Hailey's."

Without waiting for a reply, Vicky rose from the chair again and walked out of the room as both Wendy and Brian exchanged a look between them. There was something between them that was certain. They waited for the front door to close before speaking again.

"She'll be OK in a day or two," Wendy told me as she turned back to the bacon and began to pull it out of the pan.

Once breakfast was over, I headed out into the backyard, where Peanut immediately began to resume his tornado-like sprints around my feet. I found a well-worn tennis ball near the back fence and began to throw it for him. At first, he didn't want to bring it back to me, forcing me to chase him around until I managed to wrestle it from him again, but he eventually decided to switch tactics. After a few minutes of playing ball with him, I turned my attention to the rest of the yard.

Wendy had been right. Located immediately behind the backyard lay a park unlike I had ever seen. The lush green landscape stretched out in all directions, the flat ground eventually disappearing into clumps of trees circling low-lying hills. Atop one of them, I could just make out a kind of castle, no doubt some sort of tourist attraction drawing in the crowds. For me, I was more intrigued by the shadows within the trees, wondering what sort of secrets they hid from prying eyes.

"Why don't you take Peanut out for a walk and explore," Wendy called out to me when she came out with a basket of washing under one arm. "His lead is just inside the door."

"Can I?"

"Yes, of course. Brian often takes him walking along the north-bound track." Unsure of whether I understood, she pointed to the right-hand corner of the yard.

When I first opened the back gate and followed Peanut out into the world beyond, it felt like yet another level of unaccustomed freedom to me. The sky above me looked much bluer than usual, the sun burning brighter and hotter. The birdsong floating on the gentle breeze sounded like a symphony of joy, perhaps nature mirroring the mood coursing through my system.

Peanut pulled me along that path with the kind of enthusiasm reserved for excited dogs given a brief moment of freedom. He remained at the very limit of the leash, trying to drag me as fast as his little legs would allow. I could barely contain the grin on my face, and when I passed by a woman coming the other way, she gave me a strange kind of look.

"Morning," I said to her, but she didn't answer as she pulled her own dog off the path enough to give me and my hound a wide berth. I wasn't offended. I barely noticed at all, more intent on reaching the tree line where I saw a fork in the path. One way led to the main road, while the other took a sharp turn toward the nearest hill.

I don't know how far Peanut and I walked that morning, but I can tell you that we didn't stop until we reached the very top of that first hill and sat on the grass overlooking our part of the world. The little guy rested in my lap and went to sleep as I scratched the same spot behind the ears that he seemed to like so much. While I knew there was no hope of seeing it, I did spend some time looking in the direction of Whispering Hall, picturing the others sitting around on their beds, talking crap.

I didn't miss them. Nor did I miss that old life, which I barely survived. Sitting atop that hill under the shade of the only tree, I watched the world below continue on just as it had before my arrival. I could make out people going about their business in their backyards, cars and trucks driving along the web of roads. From my vantage point, it felt like I could see for hundreds of kilometres in all directions, a world utterly oblivious to the little kid who had just joined it.

"This is my life now," I whispered to no one in particular, feeling myself yearning for that conviction from the universe, for someone to confirm that I was now really a part of it. Only Peanut acknowledged my words by opening one eye and giving my hand a lick before dropping his head down again.

I must have sat on top of that hill for close to two hours before I realized I should probably get back home. It was, after all, my first day still, and I had taken somebody else's dog for a walk. The last thing I wanted was for Brian and Wendy to suspect their new kid to steal their dog and try to escape. Having the police after me on my first day was definitely not something I wanted to happen.

As it turned out, my assumption couldn't have been further from the truth. When I walked back into the house after heading back down the hill, Wendy saw me walk in while sitting at the kitchen table, sewing a skirt.

"You back already?" Her question caught me off guard.

"I just wanted to get a drink of water," was what I said, the words falling from my mouth faster than I expected.

"Help yourself," Wendy said, pointing to the sink. "There's also juice in the fridge."

"No, thanks. Water is fine," I said and grabbed myself a glass.

Freedom wasn't a concept I had actually experienced before. Not the way most people had when growing up. For me, it had consisted of either being watched at school or being watched at Whispering Hall. Time alone wasn't exactly a concept I'd grown accustomed to, not if you call a few minutes locked inside a bathroom cubicle while relieving one's self as quality time.

That day was the first time in my life when I truly understood and appreciated what it meant to be free. Not only did I take Peanut out for a walk a second time, but I made sure to remain out for most of the day, only returning just before five when I noticed the sky beginning to darken. The exploring I did...like wow, talk about mindblowing. I must have walked for absolute miles with that little dog, the pair of us searching for nothing in particular and yet feeling like we'd found heaven. And the best part was that we didn't even get anywhere near the edge of the park.

By the time I came home, both Brian and Vicky had returned as well, the latter sitting in the living room alone. Wendy was cooking dinner on the stove, with Brian sitting at the kitchen table with a beer and a newspaper.

"Make any friends during your travels?" he asked when I grabbed another drink of water, but I shook my head. "You will. There's loads of kids your age around here."

It wasn't exactly a revelation as I had seen plenty of kids hanging around a couple of the playgrounds as well as more riding their bikes up and down the many paths I'd followed. And while I did wave hello to a couple of them, my lack of confidence kept me from fully introducing myself. Each time I got near a group, I'd remember the teasing and name-calling from school and assumed I would get more of the same. I half expected them to begin chanting Rag Brigade over and over while pointing at me.

"Maybe tomorrow," I told Brian before taking my drink into the living room where Vicky was watching some show about a doctor who traveled through time in a police station called the Tardis.

It took more than ten minutes of me sitting there before she actually acknowledged me. Vicky seemed like a nice enough girl, but she came across as somewhat distracted, which I assumed some would have mistaken for arrogance.

"Do you like science fiction?" she asked me when the episode finished, and while I wasn't sure what she meant, I nodded my head anyway. "What shows do you like?"

I wanted to answer her but the question had thrown me, not only because I wasn't sure what a science fiction show was but also because I didn't want to sound dumb. Being in a new house was nerve-wracking enough, but to think that any answer might determine our future relationship scared me.

"Which ones do you like?" was what I asked instead.

"Dr. Who is my favorite, but I also like a bit of Star Trek, I guess. Brian has a collection of old '60s movies that are cool, too."

"Will he let us watch them?"

"Sometimes."

A second episode came on, but Wendy called us in for dinner before it got halfway through, and when I walked into the kitchen, the table had been set for four. It felt strange, in a nice kind of way, to take my seat at a table with a family I barely knew and yet was now a part of. Nobody looked at me any differently, and neither did my place setting. I had the same cutlery, the same glass, the same plate already stacked with food. Corned beef was what Wendy told me it was, and when she offered me some white sauce for the meat, I nodded enthusiastically.

That was the first proper meal I had ever sat down for with a real family, one that saw me as part of their clan. There was no fight to try and get enough food onto one's plate, no jostling for a seat, no struggling to keep said food for one's self. We each simply sat down and began to eat, Wendy serving each of us a drink, offering both juice and pop. I opted for the latter, my sweet tooth still very much in control of my taste buds.

When we finished our main meal, Wendy pulled an apple pie out of the oven that had been baking in the background and served it with a generous scoop of vanilla ice cream. Again, I found myself overcome with emotion, and it was hard trying to contain it. Vicky did steal a glance in my direction and smiled when she saw me trying to hide it. I didn't bother trying to stretch the experience out by reducing each mouthful of pie. There was no need to with a couple of servings still waiting in the tray for anybody wanting seconds.

I don't know whether it had been planned beforehand, but after finishing our dessert, Vicky asked whether we could all play a game of Monopoly, and when both Wendy and Brian agreed, I knew I had no choice but to join in as well. While Brian and Wendy took care of the dishes, Vicky and I set up the board, with me being given the job of handing out the money as per my new sister's instructions. I carefully created four even piles, making sure to keep each denomination separate.

What followed were two of the most fun hours of my life as we played a game I had only ever watched being played from a distance. Back at Whispering Hall, the older kids had always told me that I was too young and dumb to play it, although they did let Jeffery Lineman play, and he was two years younger than me. This time, I got to be a part of the game and actually play, and I didn't even need to partner up with anybody. Around and around the board we played, each of us buying random properties and then taking great joy in collecting rent whenever some unfortunate soul landed on our spots. The laughter is what I remember the most from that night, the sound one I hadn't ever experienced before.

That night, I ended up sleeping better than I had ever before, dropping off the second my head hit the pillow. The dream that followed took me to places where I found my mother waiting for me, her smile the perfect welcome for a son lost in the world. I don't know whether it was her way of telling me that it was OK for me to accept the love of a new family, but that is what I took out of it. As it turned out, I could have saved myself more heartache. Fate was about to revisit me in a way I could have never expected.

8

When I woke up the next morning, I did so with a renewed sense of happiness. I practically jumped out of bed, threw on the first pile of clothes I managed to grab and raced downstairs. Just as I had the previous morning, I found the rest of the family sitting at the table with breakfast in full swing. Wendy gave me a kiss on top of the head when I walked past on my way to taking my seat and pushed a bowl in front of me.

"Froot Loops?" I gave her an enthusiastic nod, and she held out the box for me.

What surprised me was seeing Vicky across from me, her face more sullen than ever. She didn't even make eye contact when I wished her a good morning, answering instead with just a bob of the head. Brian took one look at her, rolled his eyes and shook his head before turning his attention to the open newspaper lying on the table beside the plate of bacon and eggs. He didn't say anything, and I don't think it would have helped the situation.

"I'm going over to Hailey's," Vicky said as she dropped the apple she'd been holding back into the fruit bowl and pushed herself away from the table.

"Just as long as that room of yours is cleaned up by tonight," Wendy said. "And drop your washing into the basket before you go."

"I will," Vicky said almost dismissively and disappeared down the hallway before anything else could be asked of her.

"What's the matter with her?" I asked almost absently as I continued shoveling the cereal into my mouth.

"She just hasn't been sleeping well lately," Wendy said as she grabbed Vicky's empty glass. "So, what have you got planned for the day?" She looked towards the kitchen window. "Don't think the weather is going to be too kind to you today."

Looking past her, I saw what she meant. It hadn't occurred to me that the weather I'd enjoyed the previous day would be gone, and judging by the gloomy lack of sunlight through the window, I knew rain was inevitable.

"Guess I'll do some reading," I said with a shrug of the shoulders.

I refused to let the weather dampen my spirits, not after the incredible day I'd had. What I wanted was to continue that same emotional ride on Cloud 9, and nothing was going to stop it. I also hadn't spent a lot of time checking out my room and knew there would be treasures to find. Who knew what little surprises my new parents had already left in the toy box?

As it turned out, quite a few. We're talking dozens of Matchbox cars, trucks, helicopters, and planes, plus an assortment of toy soldiers and their associated weaponry. I ended up building myself an awesome little fort in the middle of my floor. I fought one megalithic battle after another, each time ending a round by dropping multiple pretend bombs from low-flying aircraft. I let my imagination go for what felt like hours on end, a kid caught up in a world only he knew.

I did end up reading as well. I found a copy of an old book called The Secret Seven: The Humbug Adventure on one of the shelves, and it didn't take me long to get lost in what felt like a classic mystery. I heard Brian and Wendy occasionally walk past my room and pause to get a look inside, but I pretended not to hear them. I think, in a weird kind of way, it made me feel better to let them think that I had settled in enough to get completely lost in a story. Or maybe it was what I really hoped they would believe.

Something that I still couldn't shake was that undeniable fear of being sent back to Whispering Hall. Now that I had essentially tasted what it meant to be taken in by a family, to be shown the world that existed outside the walls of my previous mundane existence, it made the prospect of losing it all again that much more fearful. I don't know whether I could have faced the idea of being returned to Whispering Hall now that I had experienced the other side for myself, but I knew that the possibility was very real. This wasn't some fantasy book where everyone got to enjoy a happily ever after.

When my newly-adopted mother brought me up a glass of milk and a plate of chocolate chip cookies sometime that afternoon, it only served to further instill that fear of loss into me. What I imagined most was telling a couple of the people back in Whispering Hall about the amazing life I'd been given a sample of and them immediately calling me a liar. Who could ever believe the kind of luck I must have had to land this kind of home in the first place?

"Brian will be out with his friends at the pub tonight, so Vicky and I usually order some Chinese for our dinner."

I considered the question and realized I had never had that type of cuisine before, not unless you called some soggy rice with soy sauce and a bunch of undercooked frozen vegetables Chinese.

"That sounds yum," I said, and imagine my surprise when I eventually got to taste some actual Chinese food.

The dim sims were my favorite, tiny bullets of a taste sensation that sent goosebumps down both of my arms. I think it was the salty crispiness that won it for me. We also shared a couple of chicken dishes, one with a lot of honey and the other with some kind of nuts in it. Vicky mainly stuck to the fried rice, although she did pick at a couple of bits of chicken when Wendy insisted she have some.

For entertainment, Wendy put on an old episode of Bewitched, a show about a real-life witch. I couldn't follow most of it, but each time Wendy and Vicky laughed, I did likewise in the hope of them not noticing my lack of interest. It was another one of those moments that made the home feel just a little more special to me, giving me even more reason to fear the alternative.

The three of us stayed in the living room for most of that night. After finishing our dinner, Wendy brought out a tub of ice cream and split it equally into three bowls before pouring thick chocolate sauce over the top. She then held up a small jar of something.

"Sprinkles?"

Vicky simply held out her bowl before Wendy poured a stream of colored fun onto the dessert. When she finished, I did likewise and watched my bowl come to life with even more enjoyment. An hour after finishing our ice cream, Vicky went and grabbed the half-empty box of cookies, and we munched on them while watching a movie about a huge dog named Beethoven. Now, that was a movie I could follow, and there was plenty to laugh about.

I had fun that night, *genuine* fun not like I'd experienced much before. Looking back on those times, it's funny how the most mundane of things can be so memorable. Eating dinner and watching television, or ice cream and a movie. There was nothing fancy about those moments, but the little things remain with me to this day. The way Vicky giggled whenever Beethoven caused carnage, or the way Wendy smiled when she watched us laughing. We were a family, and it is that fact that I still carry with me.

When I eventually headed up to my room after wishing the other two goodnight, I did so feeling content in a way that I knew was special. A kind of fuzziness hung over me, that sense of standing on Cloud 9 following me all the way to the bed. After taking care of my bathroom needs, I changed into some Spiderman pyjamas before climbing into bed and pulling the blanket all the way under my chin.

I was tired. My eyelids felt like they had lead weights attached to them, but no matter how many times I gave in to them and tried to drop off to sleep, my brain refused to play along. The thoughts running through my head were the kind that also made my heart race, a fear that didn't quite take the shape of something tangible.

In a way, the fear I felt didn't come from experience. I'd never been in that position before, and my fears were as much of a mystery as the adoption of my new family. Every day since arriving had been a brand new experience, and the fear of losing my new-found family was something never far from my thoughts.

I don't know how many times I closed my eyes, but at one point, I opened them to see Vicky walking down the hallway and disappearing through her door. I'm not sure whether she looked in on me first. Her room sits at the opposite end of the hallway from my own, and so I only saw the back of her. A few minutes later, Wendy climbed the stairs, shut off the bathroom light and headed back down to the ground floor where the main bedroom was located.

The minutes continued to tick by as I ended up giving in to the fact that sleep wasn't going to snatch me into its grasp, and so I rolled over, put one hand under the back of my head and stared up at the ceiling. The shadows of the outside tree branches danced with the breeze, each sliver of a darkened void pivoting back and forth. I imagined lying in my bed back at Whispering Hall, the only company during those long and lonely nights being the darkness itself.

Maybe watching those shapes moving back and forth across the ceiling had the same effect on me as counting sheep, but at some point, I think I must have drifted off. I can't tell you how much time passed by, but at some point later that night, heavy-set footsteps coming up the stairs woke me right up again. I froze, at first unsure of where I was. It took me a few moments to remember my surroundings, and once I did, I felt the phantom fingers squeezing my insides relax just a little.

While there wasn't a lot of illumination in the hallway, there was still enough coming from the skylight to let in a few rays of the moon, enough for me to make out the narrow hallway lying before me. Wendy kept a potted plant on the narrow table opposite the staircase, and it was the leaves from that miniature palm that I could make out. It took me a few seconds more to understand that those footsteps belonged to the only logical person in the house...Brian.

I don't know why, but I expected him to turn in the direction of my room the second he reached the top of the staircase, but instead, he just kind of froze, remaining perfectly still as if listening out for something. Perhaps he thought he heard a sound, some burglar roaming about the upstairs rooms and figured he'd investigate. I joined in, turning my head slightly to point one of my ears toward the doorway in the hope of helping him locate whatever he'd heard, but a few seconds later, he began to move again.

Brian didn't turn in my direction but instead turned the other way and headed towards Vicky's room. He again paused when he reached her door, and I thought that he might have heard something coming from her room. He froze again, looked over his shoulder in my direction and waited. I was about to call out to him, to tell him that I hadn't heard anything, but that was when I saw him open her door.

Up until that moment, nothing about it seemed out of the ordinary to me. I know that, on occasion, even Father Callahan used to conduct random walkthroughs of Whispering Hall, sometimes catching a random kid out of their bed and punishing them accordingly. But that was when Brian did something I couldn't understand. He opened Vicky's door, slowly crept inside her room, and then closed it again behind himself. Why would he do that?

Before I go on and tell you about the rest of what transpired that night, I need to take a moment to pause so I can share something else with you. Before deciding to write this book, I knew going in that there would be certain things I'd have to write about that might serve as triggers to certain people, incidents that may or may not trigger some repressed memories or highly volatile emotions. Triggers come in all shapes and sizes, and before I continue, I need to point out that there's a one in particular on the way.

There's no getting away from the fact that sexual abuse is part and parcel of a system designed to protect children from it. When you have a lot of children needing care on one hand and a distinctive lack of resources on the other, it opens the door for those willing to exploit the system as much as possible. It is because of the system itself that so many wards of the state end up suffering all forms of abuse at the hands of those hungry to inflict pain on the vulnerable.

At that point in my life, I was still one of the lucky ones who hadn't yet experienced the horrific shame of sexual abuse, one of the few who managed to avoid falling into the clutches of predators. I lay in my bed for quite some time, wondering why Brian would go into Vicky's room and close the door behind him. There was no logical reason for him to do so, and yet somewhere in the back of my over-inquisitive mind, something told me that it had nothing to do with hearing strange sounds in the upstairs area of the house.

When the curiosity got the better of me, I carefully climbed out of bed and stealthed my way to the very edge of my room, peering intently into the dimly lit hallway towards the other end. With nothing but the occasional creak of a floorboard breaking the silence, I wondered whether Brian and Wendy had had a fight and he had simply gone into Vicky's room to share her bed. She did, after all, have one nearly the same size as Brian's own, one far bigger than mine.

Standing in my doorway wasn't enough, and after fighting the urge to continue, my curiosity got the better of me, and I crept forward into the shadows ever so slowly. I carefully set down each foot before pausing, waiting to see whether the floorboard beneath would call out in protest and betray me in the worst way possible. It must have taken me a good five minutes to cover the same ground that would have normally taken me barely a few seconds.

When I finally reached the opposite door, I tucked myself into the wall as much as possible in case it opened again. I couldn't imagine the discomfort if Brian opened the door and found me with my ear pressed against it. What would he think or say, to find someone he'd opened his home to trying to spy on him? And yet...something about the moment continued eating away at me, willing me onward, almost as if driving me to give in to that curiosity.

I stood still next to the wall for a few moments before I leaned ever so slightly forward, just enough for my ear to reach the edge of the door. After making sure I couldn't hear the sounds of footsteps coming back towards me, I pushed my head to the right until my ear pressed against the painted timber surface, held my breath, and waited.

It took a few seconds for my hearing to adjust and then another couple of seconds to recognize what I could hear. Low, controlled sobbing was what I heard, the sound rolling through the air beyond the barrier like ripples across the surface of a lake. There was another sound too, somewhat quieter than the weeping, an almost rhythmic creaking of something I couldn't put my finger on.

It finally came to me once my underdeveloped brain finally put it together. Vicky was upset. Wendy must have told Brian once he came home, and he'd obviously gone in to try and console her. I figured it must have been because of her mother still, hence why she looked upset every so often when I saw her.

Once I thought I had figured it out, there was no reason for me to remain by the door and risk getting caught, so I slowly backed away and returned to my bed. Once I was safe under the blanket again, I promised myself to try and stay awake long enough to hear Brian leave again, but I must have lost the fight not long after. The last thing I remember was thinking that I should try and avoid asking Vicky about her mother, but the next thing I knew, I opened my eyes to find sunlight streaming in through my window and the sound of music coming from somewhere downstairs.

When I went downstairs after taking care of my bladder, I found Wendy and Brian sitting at the table alone, the latter with his usual breakfast before him. Brian also had on a business suit, the pink tie looking almost bright enough to have its own stage show on Broadway.

"Morning, sport," he said as he poured himself some extra orange juice. "How did you sleep?"

"OK, thanks," I said as I took a seat.

Vicky didn't come down for breakfast, and nobody mentioned her as I continued my mission to devour that first box of Froot Loops. Shortly after I started eating, Brian shoveled the last of the bacon into his mouth, pushed his plate away and got up.

"Alright, pet, I have to go," he said to Wendy as he gave her a kiss on the cheek. I got a little pat on the head as he walked past me, and after grabbing his briefcase, Brian left for work. I still didn't know what he did, and with my focus fully trained on the bowl of cereal before me, I forgot to ask.

Wendy eventually sat down at the table with me and began asking me all sorts of questions about the one thing I knew was coming...school. She told me that she was OK with me having that first week off so I could get used to my surroundings, but there was no getting out of the fact that I'd need to start sooner or later. She was telling me about one nearby when Vicky finally came downstairs.

"Morning, love," Wendy said to her, but rather than answer her, Vicky went to the cupboard, grabbed herself a glass, and poured herself some orange juice.

The look on her face wasn't one I'd seen on her before, the hatred in those eyes giving me chills. Wendy didn't seem to notice and continued with her description of the school. The air itself felt as if it suddenly took form, the tension thick enough to hang heavy. I suddenly felt extremely uncomfortable in the room, but Wendy just kept talking, even as Vicky finished her drink and walked out again.

It wasn't until much later, while heading out of the backyard with Peanut, that I found her sitting on the other side of the back fence leaning against it with her back. She glanced in my direction when she heard the gate open and close but quickly turned her face away. It took me just a split second to see that she was crying, and that was when I knew I had to find out why.

"Are you alright?"

"Go walk your dog, squirt," Vicky said as she tried to turn her head even further away from me.

"But you're upset, and I want to help."

"You can't help me. *Nobody* can help me."

"I can't help if you won't tell me what's wrong."

"Just go," she said, and I watched her try to wipe the tears from her eyes.

I could have done as she asked and just walked away, taken Peanut and left her alone to fight whatever battles she had going on in her head. Maybe I should have. And yet I couldn't. Something made me not only walk a little closer but also sit cross-legged a few feet away from her. I pulled Peanut in close to me to stop him from jumping onto Vicky the way he always wanted to.

"Fine," I said. "Then I'll just sit with you, and we can listen to the grass grow."

"Listen to the grass grow?" That was when she turned slightly to look at me. "How can you listen to the grass grow?"

"You can't; that's the point. But I wanted you to say something, and now you have, so I guess I win."

I expected her to yell at me, to tell me to go away and stop bothering her, but instead, the hardness of her expression melted away ever so slightly. She even managed a grin and a slight chuckle.

"Stand-up comedian, huh?"

"Maybe one day. But today, I'd rather be the little brother who wants to hear about your problems."

Again, she looked at me with that grin, although it did lessen slightly when our eyes met. There seemed to be a certain hint of shame behind it, only visible for the smallest of moments.

"Trust me, Jack. You don't want to know about my issues."

I might have only been eleven years old, but that didn't stop me from recognizing that she had grown-up kind of problems, the kinds normally not shared with kids. What I knew was that sometimes, even kids had to set aside their immaturity and try to step into boots much bigger than their own. That was the day that I had to try and become the *bigger* brother.

"I may not know the answers, but sometimes just talking about things with someone else is enough to help," was what I said, and when she looked at me, I could see that my words surprised her.

"How did you get to be so smart, huh?"

Goosebumps broke out and raced across my skin as a moment of deja vu washed over me. A momentary glimpse from the past flashed into my mind and disappeared just as quickly as an image of Ritchie Blanton shot in and out in a heartbeat. His words were what continued echoing in my head, rising and falling in perfect harmony with those of Vicky. It sounded like a reflection of time itself, the two of them positioned almost perfectly before me and speaking in perfect unison.

"Jack, what's wrong?"

"Huh?"

"You look like you just saw a ghost," Vicky said and leaned forward as she held a hand out. "Come...sit with me."

After moving Peanut aside, I slid over the final couple of feet and sat next to Vicky, our backs leaning against the fence. As if needing to protect me in some way, she swung an arm over my shoulders and behind my head, half-tucking me under. Peanut walked in a circle a couple of times, decided any spot would do, and collapsed beside my leg before going to sleep.

That was the first time in my life that I felt a part of someone else's world. I wish I could have sat in that place forever, held by someone I never imagined wanted me to be a part of her life. Up until that moment, I'd just assumed Vicky had only been polite to me, maybe following instructions from Wendy and Brian to be nice. Sitting beside her at that moment changed everything.

I don't know whether it was love, but I definitely felt myself drawn to her, wanting to protect her as much as she now protected me. I had never felt what it meant to have a brother or a sister before, and while I knew we weren't actual siblings, somehow, I believed we were even closer than that. We didn't have the blood connection. We weren't automatically bonded together because of a common family.

No, what we had went much deeper than that. Vicky came from the same part of the world I did, a world where kids needed to survive on more than just kinship. We had to fend for ourselves, often caught alone out in the real world with nobody else looking out for us. While I didn't know Vicky's past per se, I didn't need to. I sensed it just by being close to her, that protective shield we all kept to guard ourselves, hard to miss.

That was when I knew I had to tell her about my previous night's experience. There would never be a better time to ask about her pain, so I decided it was then or never.

"I heard you crying last night," I first whispered before looking up at her.

"When?"

"Late last night after Brian went in your room." She looked at me, her mouth hanging open with surprise. "I'm sorry, I know I should have been asleep, but I heard him coming up the stairs, and it woke me."

"Jack...I..."

"I don't know what it must be like living without your mum, but mine died, and I can tell you, that pain never goes away."

"Living without my mum? What are you talking about?"

"Isn't that why you were crying? Wendy kept telling me that you're upset because of your mother."

"Why do you think Brian came to my room?"

"Because you were crying." I began to feel a hint of embarrassment. "Didn't he come to see you to try and..."

I never got to finish the question. The look on her face was enough to tell me there was more to it than what I'd been assuming. Pain, shame, whatever it was staring back at me, it wasn't good.

"Jack, he didn't come to my room to help me. He came to...he came to use me."

I didn't know what she meant, but it didn't matter. Her tone was enough to tell me that it wasn't a good thing, and when she stared off into the distance, I could see that I hadn't helped the situation at all. Instead of asking her what she meant, I followed her gaze to where a woman walked by with her huge German Shepherd walking at his leash's maximum reach. She was tiny in comparison, and if the dog had made the slightest attempt to run off, I doubt she would have had the strength to stop him. I pictured her flying behind the racing dog like a balloon caught on a train, its string the only thing keeping it from shooting off into the air.

Maybe I should have asked her what she meant, but the truth is, I didn't want to know. I'd already faced plenty of my own pain during my lifetime, and this new home wasn't a place I had ever imagined finding more.

"You're lucky," Vicky eventually said. "He won't hurt you."

"How do you know?"

"Because you're not a girl." She could see that I still wasn't following, but instead of...you know...explaining it to me, she chose to skip the conversation entirely. "And I'll make sure he will never hurt you. I'll stop him if he tries."

As if wanting me to feel her words as well as hear them, Vicky pulled me in just a little closer and tightened her arm around my shoulders. We continued sitting there, watching the world pass by without ever hearing the grass grow. If I had known that would be our last day together, I might have denied Peanut the walk he so desperately wanted once he woke up, but fate doesn't come with warnings. If it did, who knows how boring our lives would become.

9

That night, we again had dinner without Brian who, according to Wendy, had a business dinner he needed to attend with some of his colleagues. This time, Wendy gave me the decision for what we would have, and I knew exactly what I wanted the moment she offered me the decision.

"Pizza," I said with the biggest grin I could muster.

"Pizza?" Wendy considered my answer and smiled. "I think I could go for some Pizza myself. Why don't you run upstairs and ask your sister what she fancies?"

Vicky asked for a plain cheese pizza, which ended up tasting better than my pepperoni one. The great thing was that Wendy set all three pizzas on the kitchen table, and we just kind of helped ourselves to whatever we wanted. It was awesome not having to fight others to get a piece, and I ended up eating way more than I should have, my stomach eventually feeling ready to explode by the time I finally gave in and quit.

"I hope you left room for ice cream," Wendy told us when she got up off the couch and went into the kitchen. By then, the three of us had demolished all but three slices of the pepperoni, a fair accomplishment, I thought.

What surprised me was just how much room I thought I had left once I saw the bowl of ice cream Wendy held out to me when she came back in the living room. There was no resisting that chocolatey gooey goodness, and the grin she gave me when I pretended to weigh up my options was enough to make Vicky laugh.

"OK, I'll have some," I said, giving in to temptation.

The ice cream didn't stand a chance, not once I got my rhythm going and ignored the uncomfortable pressure continuing to rise in my insides. I managed to consume both scoops with ease and took pride in running the spoon through the diminishing pool of syrup in the bottom of the bowl. Wendy half-applauded my effort once I handed her back the bowl.

"I've always been a sucker for the sprinkles, myself," she whispered with a bemused grin.

That night, I went to bed more or less feeling content with my life. The conversation with Vicky from earlier in the day had essentially fallen into the back of my mind, and when we wished each other goodnight, Vicky threw in an extra hug before she disappeared into her room. Wendy also came up, checked whether I had enough blankets and then kissed my cheek before turning my light off.

"Sleep tight, kiddo," she whispered to me before making her way back downstairs.

Given the crappy sleep I had the previous night, as well as then spending the afternoon chasing a crazy dog around the park, I was more than a little beat. My eyes threatened to drop out of their sockets if I didn't give in to the fatigue, and I must have drifted off almost immediately, because the next thing I knew, I found myself caught between a moment in a dream and the real world, brain fog keeping me from knowing how much of each sensation as real. My eyelids felt like they were nailed down, and it took an enormous effort for me to open them enough to see the dancing shadows on the ceiling.

What I didn't know at the time, nor even before going to sleep in the first place, was that I had subconsciously switched on a kind of detection program, some part of my brain remaining activated while the rest joined me in whatever dream world I found myself in. That small piece of subconscious awareness is what pulled me from my sleep the moment it heard the familiar footsteps again making their way up the stairs the way they had the previous night.

That strong sense of deja vu is what kept me frozen in place as Brian again stopped at the top of the stairs to listen, only this time, I knew what he was listening for. It was me, to see whether I was still fast asleep, like he hoped. While Vicky didn't tell me exactly what he had been doing to her, I wasn't naive to the whole sex thing between boys and girls. I'd heard enough of the whispers and snickering coming from nightly get-togethers between a lot of the kids at Whispering Hall, and it was their words I built my suspicions on.

What might have been only seconds felt like hours as a whitewash of emotions flooded my system, more so as Brian resumed his trek to Vicky's room. This home, this family, had become mine, a place where I honestly thought I could finally live the life I'd always dreamed about. Little did I know that the secrets hidden beyond my awareness would quickly unravel my existence within the household.

When I heard the door slowly creak open and a muffled voice speak delicately into the night air, I knew that Brian had reached his objective. I couldn't make out whether the voice was his or Vicky's but realized it didn't much matter. His intentions were clear, and I don't think her not being awake would have changed his mind. The only time I moved was when I heard the door slowly creak closed again, raising my head to see if I could hear whether Brian had actually gone into the room or was still standing outside it.

Panic hit me when I realized Brian had gone into the room, and I slid out of bed so fast, my feet tangled in the blanket, and I nearly fell to the floor in a heap. I just managed to save myself by rolling to the right and grabbing the edge of the bedhead. The beating in my chest rose considerably once I was sure I wouldn't trip up again, and somewhere on the back of my neck, a strange prickling sensation began to rise as I headed for the door. This weird sense of duty came over me, a deep-seated protective streak waking up for the first time.

Somewhere during those first few strides, I broke into a run, suddenly picturing all sorts of torturous visions in my head. I remembered those painful sobs from the previous night and couldn't imagine Vicky being forced to go through them again, not after I saw the pain in her eyes earlier that day. By the time I reached the door, I had accelerated into a near sprint.

I pushed the door handle down and bodyslammed it open at speed, my hand instinctively reaching for the light switch as I entered the room. My fingers missed, but given that I had the agility of a frightened rabbit, I slowed down enough to make a second attempt before my feet slid to a halt.

"What the -" I heard Brian start to say as the room lit up, and what I saw immediately chilled me to the bone.

Because of how much I know descriptions of sexual abuse can trigger people, I'm not going to go into descriptive details about what lay before me, but I'm pretty certain you can picture it for yourself. My entrance caught Brian off guard, and it took a few seconds for his drunken brain to catch up. When it did, I saw death in his eyes, and they had me in their sights.

"GET THE HELL OUT OF HERE, BOY," he roared as he pushed himself off the bed. He hadn't pulled his trousers all the way off, and with his feet still stuck inside them, they now betrayed him as he went stumbling towards me. I easily sidestepped him and swung a fist as his head swished past me. It caught him just behind the ear and hurt like an absolute shit when my knuckles crunched against his skull but it felt damn good.

"I'll HAVE YOU!" he screamed as he hit the edge of Vicky's dresser, and that was all the time he needed to get his bearings straight. When I tried to send a second punch into his face, Brian easily caught my fist with one meaty palm and pulled me towards him.

What happened next can only be described as an unequaled melee of epic proportion, the two of us slugging it out as Vicky began to scream for us to stop. I stood no chance, of course. My feeble attempts at inflicting damage were merely brushed aside with little effort. Brian, on the other hand, wasn't taking prisoners. His punches

not only found their mark with ease but also battered my insignificant body without mercy. His fists peppered my face and body as he
drunkenly took his anger out on the smallest opponent of the house.

I didn't see when Vicky eventually jumped on his back to try and
stop him or when Wendy charged into the room and began hitting
her husband with Vicky's pillow. Those bits would be told to me later.
By then, my eyes had already closed over, thanks to the bruising
continuing to bloom across my face and body courtesy of my so-
called father. The screams were about the only things I could focus
on, but the real challenge for me was knowing whether they were
mine or someone else's.

At some point, I passed out completely because the next few
hours are nothing more than flashes of memory. A stranger's face
leaning down close to me asking whether I was OK; me slowly
floating through the living room surrounded by yet more strangers,
sirens sounding; a pinching sensation on the back of my left hand. I
do remember riding in the back of an ambulance because I can still
vividly remember the lady asking if I knew whether I was allergic to
something.

It wasn't until much later that the real memories resumed. I woke
up in a strange room, in a strange bed, watched over by a strange
woman who kept trying to fasten something to my arm. The nurse
didn't smile when she saw me wake, her bedside manner being that
of a brick.

"Hold still while I take your blood pressure," was all she said to
me, and I remember my mouth refusing to respond when I tried to
answer her.

There was this weird buzzing somewhere nearby that felt like it
wanted to climb into my brain. When I tried to raise a hand to my ear
to try and block the sound, my arm felt like it wanted to float off on its
own, separated from the body trying to control it. My brain tingled
with shivers that rolled from the top of my head to the tips of my toes,
like slow, rhythmic waves of energy.

The idea that I had been pumped full of painkillers never
occurred to me; the concept was still as foreign to me as the rest of

the world's vices. It was only when I saw the tiny tube coming out of a bandage on the back of my hand leading up to the small plastic pouch suspended above my bed that I wondered whether that might have had something to do with it.

Someone did eventually come and see me, but it wasn't until much later in the day, after whatever drugs I'd been given had worn off and the throbbing agony of broken ribs set in. It was a woman I recognized as being the one who was at Whispering Hall when Brian and Wendy came to pick me up. The smile she'd worn that day had long vanished, replaced by a look that I wish I could have called empathy but wasn't. It was a sternness I recognized, the instant dismay of what I was about to be told foreshadowing which direction my day was about to take.

"How are you, Jack?"

"My insides hurt," I said, surprised by how composed my voice sounded.

"Yes, I'm sure they do, given the beating you took." I thought I detected an empathic smile forming, but it never took shape. "Unfortunately, I have some bad news. Mr. and Mrs. French have made the decision to end your stay with them. They've asked for you to be returned to your previous housing allocation."

She tilted her head in a way that reminded me of Peanut when he first heard me whisper his name. I thought she was waiting for me to answer, but rather than wait for me to say something, she instead gave my hand a subtle squeeze, turned around and just walked out. All I could do was watch as she left me alone to deal with the news in my own way, news that effectively dropped me back into the throes of misery.

I could have screamed, I guess, or better still, thrown the near-full glass of water on the table next to me against the wall. I could have torn the tube out of my hand, started punching the walls, maybe picked up the drip holder and thrown it through the window. God knows I wanted to. The pain in my ribs paled in comparison to the pain in my soul, the tears building and falling in great streams that ran down both sides of my face. When I knew there was no fighting it,

I carefully rolled over, ignoring the bolt of agony shooting through my middle, buried my damaged face into the pillow and sobbed. There was no point fighting it. The decision had already been made, and no amount of protesting would change it.

That afternoon, I relived my worst fears over and over, the nightmarish thoughts only broken by nurses coming in for their half-hour checks. When they brought in a tray of food for dinner, I didn't even look at it, and they took it away again just an hour later without a word. It was another indication of just how little they cared about me. The world as I had seen it for so long was back.

It must have been some time just before midnight when I did get something of a surprise, though, and not one I could have ever imagined possible. I had been lying with my back to the door to try and block out the bright fluorescent light from the corridor. Despite one of the nurses pulling the curtain across my only view of the outside world, I pulled it back just enough to give me a narrow view of a nearby building. It was that lit-up building I'd been staring at for the better part of an hour when a voice suddenly whispered to me from behind.

"Thought I'd come and check out the warrior for myself," the voice said, and when I turned over, I found Vicky standing just a couple of feet from my bed.

"Where did you come from?" She pointed at the wall opposite my bed.

"Next door. They got me cooped up with some old lady." She looked around my room. "At least you got the place to yourself." She walked closer and sat on the edge of the bed. "How are you feeling? I can't believe you did that for me."

"I couldn't bear the thought of him hurting you again," I said. I tried to sit up a little and had to bite down hard to stop a yelp of pain.

"Well, the good news is that because you did what you did, I've also been taken out of the house. My mum had promised to quit drinking, and she's going to try and take me back home."

"That's awesome news," I said, feeling genuine relief for her.

"Yeah, well, let's wait and see if she can actually go through with it this time," Vicky said, and I noted the lack of conviction in her voice. Something told me that this wasn't the first time such a promise had been made to her. "Hopefully, I can finally get some peace again, hey?"

As if sensing our paths slowly reaching a point where they would drift apart, Vicky moved into the bed a little more, sat next to me and put an arm carefully around my shoulders. I leaned in as much as I could and felt the warmth of her body next to mine. Just as she had the previous day, my first-ever big sister took me under her wing and made me feel a closeness that nobody else could ever hope to replicate. We sat together like that for more than an hour, the pair of us needing each other's comfort and giving it back just the same.

When the nurse came to do her rounds a little after one that morning, she not only ended our brief moment of bonding but also our relationship as a whole. She ordered Vicky back to her room, and the smile my sister gave me when she turned back one final time near the door is the last image I have of her. I never saw her again. Just two weeks after getting out of the hospital, her mother managed to convince the state that she'd amended her ways and regained custody of her only child. Two days later, on the morning of her fourteenth birthday, Vicky died in a house fire after her mother left a candle burning in her room that she'd been using while drinking bourbon in bed. I still miss my big sister to this day, hoping that she finally found the peace she'd been hoping for.

10

The day I left the hospital to return to Whispering Hall, a thunderstorm rolled across the greater London area with enough destruction that multiple roads ended up blocked due to fallen trees. I honestly believed that fate had sent it, trying to delay my return while it looked for alternative options for me. Unfortunately, it failed, and two hours after climbing into the car with Alison Farrow, we pulled up out the front of Whispering Hall, my journey having come full circle.

The moment I climbed out of the car, I could hear snickering coming from one of the upstairs windows. I didn't dare look up, doing my best to avoid any sort of eye contact with those who would gleefully cheer my return. That was the thing with the others at Whispering Hall. Nobody really wanted to see anybody else succeed out in the real world. Jealousy was perhaps one of the most common traits amongst the population, which meant it was every kid for himself.

Once inside, the induction process took just minutes, if you could even call it that. Father Callahan simply welcomed me back, ruffled my hair with one hand and squeezed my shoulder with the other before pointing me to the stairs.

You know the drill," were the only words of encouragement, and I hadn't even reached the staircase before both he and Alison Farrow disappeared into his office.

A waiting party stood at the top of the stairs, and they made it pretty clear how they felt about my return. A few began to cheer and clap the second I came into view, while the rest of the group waited until I walked back into the hall itself before making their feelings known. Failure was seen as a win for the group, two opposing sides in a game nobody ever wanted to truly play in the first place. If I failed, then that opened up the possibility of someone else gaining a place in a home, unless, of course, the home itself turned out to be cancelled completely like the French's.

"Even got your old bed ready for you," Bruce Martin howled once the others eased up a bit, and sure enough, waiting for me near the back row, two from the left sat my bunk, the bottom one's mattress rolled up as if waiting for me.

I think the worst part for me wasn't so much returning to Whispering Hall, nor losing my home with Brian and Wendy. For me, the worst part was the lack of anybody asking me about my injuries. It wasn't as if they'd healed during my short stint in the hospital. Sure, my eyes had fully opened again, but the previous purple bruises had turned into dirty custard-like stains on my face, the grotesque patches a constant reminder of that night. Nobody could have missed them, and given the way people's eyes seemed to gravitate down towards them whenever they spoke to me, it was clear they made them uncomfortable.

I was essentially back in a world of one, a place where the only true person who existed was me. Everyone else was just a stranger caught within *their* world, each of us trying to survive as best we could. Sure, some had friends, or so they believed, but that friendship only stretched as far as their willingness to tolerate the other person. I'd seen plenty of fights erupt over the most petty things, those solid friendships falling apart faster than a house of cards in a storm.

Given it was a Saturday when I returned, I ended up having the whole weekend to get back into the swing of things. By Monday morning, Father Olsen had re-enrolled me into school, and I attended along with the rest of my fellow Rag Brigaders. A couple of people did ask where I'd been for the previous week, but when I answered, I could tell they weren't really interested, and so I let it slide.

The thing is, I struggled in a way I hadn't yet experienced before. Prior to going to the French's home, I had nothing to compare my existence to. What I had experienced back in the days of living with my mother had all but vanished from my memories. The passage of time had effectively robbed me of my childhood memories, and what remained was nothing more than a collection of brief flashbacks, each a bare sliver of recollections.

In the years since those days, I heard a saying about love that I immediately adjusted to fit my narrative because it opposed my thoughts exactly. It's better to have loved and lost than never to have loved at all. To me, the reverse was true, only instead of love, it was life itself. Now that I had tasted what true freedom really felt like, I couldn't bear going back to what I was before. My individuality, my privacy, my identity, it had all been stripped away just as fast as it was gifted to me, the taste of losing it far more painful than I could ever imagine.

Those first few nights must have been some of the toughest of my life. I know I keep saying that, but for the most part, it's true. I seriously struggled to adjust back into life inside Whispering Hall that second time. The depression tended to fill me the moment I woke up and wouldn't subside again until the moment sleep finally showed me some mercy at night. The hours in between? Pure torture.

If it hadn't been for a new kid arriving about three months after my own return, who knows how long I would have remained in that secluded shell of mine, but once Melvin Kent showed up, everything changed. He was a couple of years older than I was, and it was obvious from the moment I saw him that the poor kid was in for a rough ride. The huge buckteeth he sported were just the start of an entire production of things the others got to pick on. Big ears, near cross-eyed with these huge bug eyes that sat behind thick horn-rimmed glasses, the slight stagger in his walk, the lisp he spoke with. Take your pick. Each kid that met him did, sometimes groups pointing out all his flaws at once.

It was as if by fate, Melvin had ended up in the bottom bunk next to my own. He moved in during a particularly quiet moment in the hall, as most kids had gone downstairs to kick the ball around outside. I remained indoors, of course, happily keeping company with myself. Only one other kid had been there with me, one of the oldest who had gotten himself engrossed in some book he'd brought back from the school library.

"I'm Melvin, but my friends call me Mel," this new kid said as he dropped his bag on the bunk. He went as far as to hold out his hand, and I had little choice but to shake with him. Something about his smile made me feel sorry for him, although I silently questioned whether he actually had any friends, much less those who would call him Mel.

"Jack," I said as we shook hands to confirm the introduction, and then, trying to draw a grin, I added, "but my friends call me Jack."

It took Mel a moment to get the joke, but once he did, he began laughing and shaking his head.

"That's a good one," he said as he waggled a finger at me. "I can see I'm going to have to watch you." He set himself up on the bed, unbagged a bunch of clothes, which he dropped into a couple of spare drawers, and then sat cross-legged on the mattress while staring at me.

For a minute, we just sort of hung in a suspended kind of silence, neither of us really talking but not doing anything else to draw attention away. Before Mel's arrival, I had simply been lying on my back, staring up at the bottom of the bed above mine while daydreaming. That had pretty much been how I'd spent all of my spare time. Mel's arrival hadn't exactly changed my plans, but it did feel unnatural to continue doing nothing while being stared at by a complete stranger.

"I'm going to guess that you're eleven," he suddenly said while pointing at me.

"Lucky guess," I said.

"OK, now guess my age, then."

"No, I don't want to."

"Go on, just guess," Mel said, and I don't know why, but for some reason, I couldn't stop grinning as he continued trying to convince me to guess his age. It was such a stupid game, one with very little purpose.

But instead of just giving up and dropping it, this kid just continued at me, wanting me to guess his age like some ridiculous baby game.

"Go on, Jack, guess it," he'd whisper before chanting the words over and over again, to the point where even Sam looked up from his book and considered telling the newcomer to shut it.

"Ten," I whispered after holding out for as long as possible. It was only when I heard some of the others coming back up the stairs that I felt an urgency to shut him up before they heard him. Like I said before, Whispering Hall isn't a place known for warm welcomes.

"Hey, check out the new kid," I heard Arty Fowler call out once he reached his own bunk, the nine-year-old one of those annoying little brats who always needed to be the centre of attention.

It took just under a minute for a group of about fifteen boys to build a half-circle in front of our bunks, the new kid the latest zoo exhibit for the group.

"Hey, what's your name, four eyes?" Buster Clements said, and then absorbed the chuckles from the others with glee.

"Check out those glasses," someone else called out.

"I swear I saw that same disguise in a MAD mag the other day," this kid called Nute Haggerty called from the back. He had this annoying habit of smacking everyone on the back whenever he dropped a funny line. The rest of his crew just about broke up with laughter.

Despite all of the negative attention and insults, I watched this new kid who looked skinnier than a broom handle weather the attack like a seasoned warrior. Not once did he show the slightest sign that he was offended, or scared, or even insulted by the slew of words thrown at him. Each attack came and went with seasoned precision, and he simply sidestepped them all, at one point grinning before gesturing for the insults to continue.

"Keep them coming, guys, keep them coming," that gesture seemed to say and while a couple of the boys tried to accept the challenge, the majority of them decided that they had enough and turned their attention to the gaming corner where a couple of others had already set up a new Mortal Kombat challenge.

Believe it or not, but that display of unbridled courage I had just witnessed left me dumbfounded. No, not just dumbfounded but outright speechless. I just sat there with my jaw hanging open as I watched the usual frenzy fall away, each kid shaking their head in disgust before turning away and heading off. When we were alone again, Mel leaned a little closer in my direction.

"That's how you win every time," he whispered. "Just go with the flow."

"But they called you names. Made fun of your appearance."

"So?" He chuckled and shook his head. "Know what you are, kid, and nobody can use it against you."

I was stunned by his courage and, more so, impressed with how easily he fended off a full-frontal assault from an experienced crew. It wasn't exactly hero worship, per se, but I can tell you with a hand on my heart that I immediately found myself respecting the new kid in Bunk 4A. He'd opened my eyes to a different side of Whispering Hall warfare, and I intended to learn everything I could from him if only he'd hang around long enough to teach me the rest of his ways. As it turned out, two weeks was all I had.

Like so many others before him, Melvin Kent ended up in Whispering Hall as a victim of circumstances. His mother had died during childbirth, three months after his father skipped out on his twenty-something-year-old pregnant girlfriend. At first, Melvin found himself in the care of his paternal grandmother, but she too passed away just a year later, leaving him an orphan in every sense of the term. After working his way from one boarding home to another, he eventually ended up with a family with whom he lived for close to six years before their circumstances changed and he was forced back into the system.

For the two weeks he remained at Whispering Hall, Mel never lost that fighting spirit of his. Not once. I watched the others try time and again to break him, their insults growing darker and meaner with each attempt, but he calmly deflected them as easily as he had that initial attack. We didn't exactly grow close during his brief time there, but we did form a kind of friendship that involved him opening up to me a couple of times. I think he did it as a way of opening me up, because for whatever strange reason, I too found myself wanting to share my life story with him, something I had never done with anybody before.

Hindsight is a beautiful thing, and I guess it wouldn't surprise you to learn that these days, Mel is better known as Dr. Melvin Kent, one of the most sought-after psychologists in Britain. I once caught up with him in a Manchester book shop. He'd been invited into the place as part of his book tour, and I just happened to find myself standing in line with his latest publication tucked under one arm. He even added a little message above his autograph, a message meant as a reminder of a time where we shared what little we had in a place we'd both rather forget. *Guess my age, Jack,* was what he wrote, and as I sit here writing this part of the story, I'm looking over at the bookshelf where his message to me continues to bring a smile to my face.

When Mel eventually left Whispering Hall, he did so with his head held a lot higher than when he first arrived. I was one of the few who made sure to see him off, standing at the window while watching him follow his uncle and aunt out through the gate. He turned back one final time when he reached the Range Rover's rear door and gave me a wave. As I returned it, he shouted the best advice I'd ever received.

"They can't hurt you if you know what you are," was what he called out, and I gave him a thumbs-up just to be sure he knew I had heard.

Nobody else stood with me that day, Mel's departure my own to watch. He became the third person to have a significant impact on my life. Our time together may have only been brief, but the depth of our bond could never be broken. Little did I know that the closest bond I'd ever have with someone would turn out to be two people, and once I met them, nothing in my life would ever be the same.

11

There exist certain dates in my life that came to represent certain moments which I saw as significant events. My mother's birthday, my mother's death, Vicky's death, Ritchie's death, Melvin Kent's departure, my first arrival at Whispering Hall, my meeting with Elizabeth Hampstead. All the dates that I saw as pivotal moments within my otherwise mundane existence. When I first woke up on March 24, 1999, I had no idea that the day would turn out to be something significant. Few days rarely did, I guess. It wasn't as if fate would announce itself with a warning, although it would have certainly helped.

The only thing that did matter was that it just happened to be my 13th birthday, a day that meant just one thing to a kid having a birthday...they got a cake with candles after dinner. Sometimes, a kid might even get a present or two, but those would normally be nothing more than things the others had either made in craft classes at school or had managed to steal and smuggled into the place. Even then, it might only be some rusted old pocket knife or an old yo-yo.

What should have alerted me to the fact that something else was stirring in the winds was the fact that Father Callahan hadn't asked me about the cake the previous evening during his final walkthrough. His routine usually involved walking amongst the bunk beds, pausing next to whoever's birthday was the next day and asking them their preferred type of cake. It never occurred to me at the time that because of his sudden departure the previous evening when Father Callahan was called to nearby St. Luke's for some unknown emergency, my choice of cake was effectively skipped.

Only when I woke up on the morning of my birthday did I remember the routine and how it had differed. And since nobody else really cared about my birthday, it wasn't a matter that needed bringing up. I, as you might have guessed, wasn't one of the ones to receive any kind of gifts; the cake was often the only indication that it was my birthday at all. I didn't care, of course. By then, I'd gotten used to how the world viewed me, and I figured that if it left me alone, then I would do likewise.

The first real indication that something was up was when Father Callahan came to the hall and asked me to head downstairs with him. At first, I had wild visions of me being found guilty of some crime I hadn't committed. Being brought down to the office normally only meant one thing... disciplinary action, the other reason too rare for anybody to really consider. Halfway down the stairs was when he dropped the bombshell.

"Jack, there is a family waiting in my office who think they might have a home for you."

The revelation just about gut-punched me, and by the time we reached the bottom of the staircase, I could barely breathe. For two years, I had silently prayed to be given another chance with a family, and now, after all those endless nights of whispering into the darkness, it appeared as if fate had finally answered my call. Father Callahan briefly stopped before we reached the door and turned to me.

"Now, listen, young man. I want you to know that you don't have to feel obliged to go with these people. You're now old enough to be able to choose for yourself. Mrs. Farrow and I have had a good chat with this couple, and we believe they will make for a wonderful family with you."

Father Callahan was right. From the moment I met Roger and Kay Preston, I felt like I'd known them forever. They radiated this warmth that kind of enveloped a person, drawing them in like moths to a flame. Kay had this massive smile that seemed to light up her whole face, and when we shook hands that very first time, the warmth from her touch seemed to run all the way up my arm.

While you might assume that there were moments of deja vu for me walking out of Whispering Hall with a second adoptive family, the truth is, I didn't think once about the previous time I'd made a similar journey. Aside from Vicky, there wasn't a thing I wanted to remember about that other family, a couple who had hurt us the way they had. This was an entirely new opportunity for me, a chance to rebuild a life that still struggled to feel like something I should have been proud of.

Roger turned out to be a published writer, the author of almost a dozen thrillers which he had penned over the course of the previous decade. We're not talking James Patterson kind of fame, but he apparently made enough to support the household. Kay, on the other hand, volunteered at a local nursing home three days a week and spent the rest of her time running the household.

We stopped off at this cafe for lunch on the way home, where I not only got to enjoy one of the best hotdogs I'd ever tasted, but I also got my very own chocolate cheesecake that the waitress brought out with a golden candle sitting in the middle of it. There wasn't any enormous fanfare, thank God, just a couple of well-wishes from my new parents, so to speak.

The Prestons lived about an hour away, in Hounslow, and the second I jumped out of the car, I found one of the best features of the home flying overhead. The house sat almost in direct line with Heathrow Airport, which meant that all manner of aircraft flew overhead every few minutes.

"You'll get used to the noise," Roger said as he grabbed my bag from the back.

"*If* you're lucky," Kay threw in, and I could tell from her tone that she didn't seem too pleased with the display.

I couldn't imagine not liking the chance to watch such magnificent aircraft flying so close to the ground. I must have laid on the grass in the backyard for hours that first afternoon, each time trying to make out the logos and serial numbers of the planes that passed by. Unfortunately for me, the Prestons didn't own a dog, or any pet for that matter. Kay had allergies to most types of animals, which kept their home an animal-free zone.

"Maybe if you really need a pet in your life, we could look at possibly getting you a goldfish," Kay suggested that night at dinner, and while I couldn't exactly take one for a walk down to the local park, it was better than having no pet at all.

"Sure, that would be great," I said before Roger changed the subject to matters closer at hand.

"Now, I know you're new, and Mrs. Farrow suggested we keep you home for at least the first week to help settle you in. There is a matter we need to discuss regarding chores, however." Kay rolled her eyes as the two of them exchanged a glance.

"This is all Roger, kiddo," she said as she leaned back in her chair.

"What?" Roger looked across the dining table at her and shrugged his shoulders. "My father always said a man begins growing into a responsible adult when he's young, and I always had to do chores around the house." He looked at me and pretended to be confused. "I think I turned out alright." Kay simply shook her head.

"I don't mind doing chores," I chipped in, and Roger appreciated my input.

"Well, thank you," he said with a nod of the head. "I don't mind when you do it, but the front and back grass needs mowing once a week, the weeding of the garden beds once a month. Now, I'm not expecting show-quality work, but I do expect a certain level of commitment."

"Yes, of course," I said, still struck by having never had chores before.

"And for your effort, I think we can manage a tenner a week,"

Roger finished, pulled the nominated note from his wallet and held it out to me. "Paid in advance, of course."

I was too dumbstruck to speak, unsure of whether to grab the note or admit the joke. In my mind, I could see Roger pulling it back the instant I reached for it, making this silly noise before squeezing my nose and telling me he'd got me.

"Well, go on, take it," was what he said instead and pushed it a little closer to me. "It won't bite." I looked at Kay, and she gave me an approving nod, one which I trusted far more than the offering before me.

I had money before, of course, but never an amount higher than a few coins. There was no hiding the trembling fingers when I did finally reach for it, and once in my hand, I felt the very air in my lungs had vanished.

"Geez, kid, it's just a tenner," Roger said with a grin. "If you're anything like me, it'll be gone in a day or two anyway." When I looked at him with bewilderment, he held a hand up. "Because you'll spend it," he said with a laugh. "I'm not stealing it back off you."

I lied earlier when I wrote that I couldn't compare the previous family to my new one. The truth is that I hadn't stopped the comparisons since meeting my new family. The stopping at the cafe, the conversation during the drive home, the first moment hearing a giant A380 flying just a couple of hundred metres over my new house, every minute of that afternoon had been compared to those of my previous adoption and Vicky aside, I already knew which home I preferred.

The other moment of comparison that ultimately won the day was when I eventually went to bed, completely beat after a long day of unbearable excitement. Unlike that first night when I struggled to even close my eyes at the Frenchs because of my fear of being returned to Whispering Hall, this time I felt no such anxiety. For some reason, contentment came with the territory, and I found that I felt more at ease in my new home than I could have possibly imagined.

That night, I slept better than I had during the previous couple of years, and I don't think the smile left my face for a second because I felt it still there when I woke up the next morning. The Prestons' home only had a single level, quite a lot smaller than the French's, but in a way, it felt a lot homelier, if that's even a word. I found Kay ironing a shirt on the kitchen table, and she greeted me with that same smile she had the moment we met.

"Good morning," she said as I grabbed a seat opposite her. "Are you OK with grabbing your own breakfast? I wasn't sure what you'd like, so I grabbed a few different boxes of cereal for you." She pointed to one of the cupboard doors. "Pantry is over there, and milk is in the fridge." She resumed ironing before pausing again. "Oh, and the bowls are behind that door there," she said, pointing to one of the dozens lining the kitchen.

"Thanks," I said and jumped up to see what I had to choose from.

"Rog is in his study working," Kay continued before lowering her voice. "Just be sure to keep it down when the door is closed. It means he's actually writing and not procrastinating plot points." I didn't know what she meant and so just grinned back at her but made a mental note about the request.

I didn't pay too much attention to the other boxes of cereal once I spotted the familiar toucan staring back at me from the edge of a box near the front. Healthy or not, Froot Loops still had my heart, and since I hadn't had any for quite some time, you can imagine the speed at which I ate that first bowlful.

Kay left for work before I finished my breakfast, and after completing the first load, I ended up pouring myself a second, not because I was hungry but because I was enjoying the taste just a little too much. The house sat in silence around me, with only a light humming coming from the fridge, until the very ground seemed to shake beneath my feet as one of the larger aircraft flew overhead. At that moment, I wasn't quite sure how I could ever find myself getting used to such a noise to the point where I no longer heard it. Maybe it was just a boy thing, but the sound of such raw power drew me in each and every time a plane flew overhead.

I spent the first part of the morning mostly just checking out my room, getting to know where everything was and how the TV worked. Yes, for the first time in my life, I had my very own television, which had been set up in such a position that I could easily watch it from my bed. Not only that, but the TV also had a built-in DVD player as well, and I'd already spotted a rather extensive collection of discs in the living room. Roger also OK'd me to grab whatever ones I wanted to watch when he emerged from his office mid-morning and saw me playing around with the remote control before quickly disappearing again.

By eleven o'clock, I had circled what I could of the house twice, and with Roger still cocooned in his office, I decided to head out for a bit more exploration. Something I never got to do at the French's home was get to know the actual neighborhood. Sure, I spent plenty of time running around the parkland, but the actual streets? Not so much. I knew that if I was going to try to make some genuine friends, I would need to go to where other kids hung out.

The day wasn't exactly spectacular weather-wise, with dark clouds looming near the horizon, but the rain held off as I trudged along the first couple of blocks. Every so often, a fresh roar of jet engines would draw my attention up, but four blocks from home, I got what Kay meant when other things began to draw my attention back to matters closer to ground level.

When I reached the entrance to a small non-descript park, I wasn't going to enter at first. Shyness had sometimes gotten the better of me, and I still felt uncomfortable about being the new kid in the area. What finally persuaded me to push through the fear and get my butt moving was the fact finding friends was the original purpose for me coming out in the first place.

The park appeared to be set out in the shape of a large fat bottle, the narrow neck and lid the entrance point from where I entered. Various pieces of play equipment sat right in the middle, with several park benches scattered randomly around the perimeter, along with half a dozen trees offering limited shelter from the weather. It was under one of these trees that I spotted a girl sitting alone, reading a book. Something about her appearance immediately grabbed my attention.

When going to school with my Whispering Hall brethren, it was never hard to find one of our kind because of our appearance. There was just something uniquely recognizable about a kid wearing mismatched clothes and sporting the kind of hair that lacked the normal level of care. Looking at the girl, she could have easily been mistaken for one of the Rag Brigade, her bright pink and way over-sized sweater perhaps the brightest clue of all.

I didn't aim for her to begin with. I didn't want to make it too obvious that I recognized her for what she was, or at least what I assumed she was, and so I began to work my way around the outside while watching a bunch of younger kids use the climbing equipment. The girl didn't seem to notice me, or so I thought, her eyes remaining downcast on the open book she held in her lap.

When I had passed by the girl to the point of losing sight of her behind the tree she was leaning against, I briefly paused to reassess my plan. You have to put yourself in my shoes. I was a kid of thirteen and had about as much experience with girls as a penguin with an umbrella. I had lived the majority of my life with a bunch of boys, went to a single-sex school, and had a sister for all of a week some two years earlier. At that particular moment, girls were definitely *not* my forte.

I was nervous. In my mind, I could see countless scenarios unfolding, each one more intense than the last and each one ending with all of the kids hilariously calling out my failure with wild cheers and howls. The prospect of her turning me away was not only scared the absolute crap out of me, but ultimately convinced me that I had to go through with it if I ever wanted to consider myself a Melvinator, as I used to call my old friend. I imagined him in the same scenario and could see him confidently walk up to said stranger, calmly intro-duce himself, and then quietly sit down and begin a conversation.

The moment Melvin entered the equation, I knew I couldn't back away, and after drawing in a couple of huge deep breaths, I turned to keep following the outer perimeter and willed my legs to carry me forward. When I reached the next corner, I barely slowed, sure that if I did, I'd not only stop completely but also wimp out entirely. Failure was not an option, and I could hear those exact words being spoken by Melvin somewhere inside my head.

When I eventually reached the moment of no return, that point in my journey where I ended up close enough for the girl to look up from the pages of her book because she spotted movement out of the corner of her eye, I very nearly continued straight past her. My legs felt almost on autopilot, with enough energy powering through them to carry me all the way to Scotland. What stopped me was her looking up at me, catching my gaze and speaking to me.

"Would you mind helping me up?"

"Excuse me?"

Her question had been clear, but thanks to my over-active brain, only half the words actually registered, the rest lost amongst a barrage of confusion. Instead of repeating herself, the girl simply held up a hand to me.

"Please?"

Unsure of what I was supposed to do, I let my subconsciousness take over, it activating the muscles in my arm almost on impulse. Before I knew it, I'd reached out my hand, and the girl grabbed a hold of it and pulled herself up.

"Thanks, I think my legs were starting to cramp," she said as she began stretching back and forth. Too stunned to speak, I just stood there watching her.

Other than Vicky, I'd never really touched another girl before that moment, and the interaction kind of froze me up a little. Maybe that was why the girl again seemed to take the lead by holding out her hand once more to introduce herself.

"I'm Emma."

"Jack," I said, again overcome with awkwardness but thankfully still switched on enough to follow basic courtesy. This time when our hands touched, we shook like a couple of grown-ups before taking a step away from each other again.

The thing about that physical touch isn't what you might think. It wasn't shyness or embarrassment about being touched by a girl; it went much deeper than that. The only real physical touch I had ever felt involved beatings, a lot of the time from those who were supposed to protect me. Physical abuse is probably more rampant throughout the system than the sexual kind, and yet both leave eerily similar scars. Avoiding physical contact was a way for me to protect myself from harm, the kind I felt powerless to escape from.

The idea of meeting friends wasn't a new concept to me, but the thought of meeting an actual girl who might end up as a friend wasn't something I had actively considered before that moment. Yes, I'd become curious. Show me a teenage boy who wasn't at that age. But most people already had significant experience with the opposite sex by that age. Not me. A girl, as far as I was concerned, was a strange creature of mythical proportions.

"What book are you reading?" I asked as we stood there awkwardly together.

"Oh, it's some stupid kid's thing I found in the room where I'm staying." I immediately picked up on the fact that she didn't call it her home, another indication of her connection to the Rag Brigade. "You're not from around here, are you?"

"I just moved in down the street," I said and then thought it the perfect opportunity to drop a little clue for her to pick up. "It's my new family. They just adopted me."

I cringed, hearing the words come out the way they did, not all sounding the way I had imagined them in my head, but it didn't seem to matter to her.

"You're adopted? Me too."

"I know," I said, deciding it best to come clean. "I could tell." Emma didn't miss a thing, immediately aware of our connection.

"It was the jumper, right?"

"Well, it does make you kind of stand out," I said.

"And it's like three sizes too big," she admitted. "Ugh, what I wouldn't give for just one decent jumper."

"I know how you feel," I said, pointing to my shoes. "Had these since last year when they looked like clown shoes on me."

"I was about to go for a walk. Want to come?"

"To where?" I asked.

That was when Emma looked past me to where a group of kids who had been playing began to chant something over and over again, the single word one every kid on the planet would recognize just because of the situation. Fight. About a dozen looked to have encircled two others who appeared to be in a stand-off, and I immediately zeroed in on the one who kept looking at the others and grinning.

"That's the boy I met yesterday," Emma said as she grabbed my shirt and gave it a brief tug. "Come and help me," she said before running towards the gathering.

It wasn't a sense of urgency that willed me to move, but there was definitely something at play because halfway to where the group stood, I passed by my new friend. Remembering Melvin's courage, I summoned however much I had in my own tank and took a deep breath.

"Hey, leave him alone," I called out as I reached the other edge of the circle. A couple of the smaller kids stood aside while the rest just turned to look at me.

"Oh, yeah? Who called you for backup?" the kid playing the bully role said with a smirk.

"I did," Emma said from behind me, and that was when I noticed the kid I'd stepped in to defend.

I immediately saw why Emma might have wanted to help him. Much shorter than his opponent, he could have been the brother of my old friend, Melvin Kent, sporting the same kind of glasses and teeth. Only his hair was blond and not black, and he was a bit more solid, but the rest of him fit almost perfectly.

"Look, the freak has got himself a girlfriend," the bully cried with delicious glee, immediately looking for support from his friends, who didn't let him down. A torrent of laughter and howls rose from the group as the bully turned back to his original victim. "Kissed her yet, freak?"

"I'm going to kiss *you* if you don't shut up," I said as I stepped closer. I wasn't a whole lot taller than the bully, but every centimetre counted, and a height advantage was a height advantage. I stepped close enough until our noses almost touched, and every muscle in my body tensed, ready for action. If he had made the mistake of speaking at that point, I think he knew I would have unloaded on him. I already had both my fists balled up, ready to strike. All they needed was the brain impulse to do so.

Bully considered his options as we stared off for a few seconds longer, the rest of the group watching on in silence. I could feel their hopes for a fight, and their outcries would have exploded if one of us had thrown a punch, but I could see that the bully lacked the conviction and confidence to react.

"Come on, Troy," someone behind me said. "Let's get out of here and let these babies play with each other."

I could see him seize the invitation long before he reacted, his eyes deceiving him one last time before he grinned and backed away.

"Enjoy kissing each other," he said with a snicker once he'd safely backed away a couple of feet. "Let's go," he added and gave one of his friends a slap on the chest before the rest of them turned to follow.

"Thanks," the blond Melvin said once he was sure the group had really gone and weren't coming back.

"You're welcome," I said and stuck out a hand. "I'm Jack Hardy."

"Oliver Holden, or Ollie to my friends," the kid said and shook with me before Emma stepped closer.

"I thought you were a goner for real," she said with a grimace. "I've seen that kid around. He's bad news." When she realized that she'd only given her partial name, she added, "And it's Emma Grant. Em for short."

"Well, Em for short," I said. "Thanks to you, we probably helped Ollie here getting a beating."

"Nah, I would have taken them all on," Ollie joked as he snickered with glee.

"Sure you would have," I said, calling out his sarcasm. "You're lucky you didn't end up in the back of an ambulance."

That was how I met the best friends I would ever have in this world, two non-descript kids hanging out in a non-descript park in some non-descript suburb of London. Two kids who others saw as the kind who hid in the middle of the classroom, lacking the social skills to take charge in groups due to that lack of self-confidence, which came from a feeling of both separation and isolation. Two kids whom I saw as survivors...because that's what we were.

12

E mma, Oliver, and I saw each other a lot over the coming weeks
and months, made easier by us all going to the same school.
Wilson Community School also happened to be my very first unisex
school, meaning I got to sit amongst both boys *and* girls in class. It felt
strange at first, but just like Kay had told me about the planes flying
over our house, it quickly became just another part of my day that I
barely noticed.

For the next few months, my life became something of a dream to
me. Some mornings, I'd wake up and pinch myself to make sure I was
really awake and living the life I had been dropped into. It just felt too
perfect, if that makes sense. Kay and Roger were so nice to me, always
asking whether I needed anything and then simply buying whatever
I wanted. They even bought me a Nintendo 64. Not a brand new one,
but one they found at Cash Convertors. Having never owned a
gaming console in my life, I wasn't about to argue.

Some of the best days of my life were those when Emma and
Ollie came over to my house and we played Mario Kart in my room.
The three of us would race each other for hours, only taking breaks
when Kay would drop us in a plate of freshly-baked cookies she'd
made, or better still, pizza. Ollie always ate the most, one time

managing to eat an entire pizza on his own after Em and I dared him, me throwing in all the change I had in my pocket at the time.

"Easy money," Ollie said with a delightful grin after shoving the last piece into his mouth and snatching the coins up. "Easy money."

"If it's so easy, then why do you look like you're about to barf?" Em asked as Ollie leaned back against the side of my bed, and for one nervous minute, I thought he actually might, but he managed to hold it down.

The thing about our world was that luck hadn't just struck once but three times, as far as we were concerned. Each of us had come from a history of broken homes and abandonment, victims of a system that had failed us time and again. This time, though, it appeared as if fate had finally seen fit to show us some love with proper homes and proper foster parents to care for us.

The trademark Rag Brigade indicators also began to diminish from our lives. It didn't take long for those baggy, worn-out clothes to disappear, replaced with proper fitting threads we were proud of. Sure, they weren't exactly designer gear, but given where we came from, none of us complained. We even *looked* better, our hair somehow growing out the hardship stress and replaced with shiny confidence. Surprisingly for me, I even watched the beginning stages of acne fade away completely, returning my skin to something more akin to my younger self.

One of the biggest highlights for me came in the late summer of 1999 when Roger and Kay surprised me with a trip to Bexhill, where Kay's sister owned a holiday house near the beach. The best part, though? Roger and Kay agreed for Em and Ollie to join, just as long as their parents were fine with it, which of course they were. And so, in August of that year, three weeks before we were due to return to school, the five of us headed out late one Friday afternoon and made the trip to the southern coast.

The three of us sat in the back, happier than ever, passing Ollie's Gameboy back and forth between us as we tried to better each other's scores on Tetris. Kay kept changing the songs as Roger navigated the roads, mixing the music up between Roxette, Phil Collins, and Rod

Stewart, who, according to Roger, was Kay's true sweetheart in life, something she rigorously denied while slapping Roger's hand away.

We reached Bexhill just after six and with the sun still some time from completely setting, Roger allowed us kids to head down and check out the beach, which sat just a couple of streets over. We must have run like the wind once out of view, the three of us cheering and howling into the sky as we raced each other to be first onto the sand. I won, of course, being the fastest out of the three of us, but Emma came quite close after I got held up by an old woman walking her dog, some small white thing that looked more like a rabbit.

The beach wasn't exactly like those you might find on postcards showing some divine tropical island, but it served its purpose just the same. Instead of sand, it had pebbles, and instead of beautiful white-topped waves rolling in, the surface of the water looked almost flat, with the murky wavelets appearing to gently lap at the edges of the beach.

Ollie, being the clown of the group, didn't slow down once he reached the beach. Instead, he raced right through where Emma and I stood waiting for him and continued on towards the water while shouting "Tally-ho" at the top of his lungs in a voice that sounded like a Scotman trying to imitate an Indian. He cheered with this ridiculously crazy voice he always put on when trying to be funny and began to skip towards the edge of the beach. I thought he might stop when he reached the edge, but not even the water slowed him.

He jumped right in, clothes and all, bounding through huge splashes for a few metres before the water level reached his hips, at which point he comically collapsed and disappeared beneath the surface. When he reappeared, he did so by jumping up as hard as he could, thrusting his fists into the air and beginning to cheer all over again. All Emma and I could do was stand there enduring fits of laughter, the pair of us close to falling over as we watched Ollie, through tears streaming down our faces, thrash about like a drowning psycho. People walking by stopped to stare at him before shaking their heads and continuing on.

"What are you guys waiting for?" he shouted after dunking

himself a second time and emerging even more energetic than before as he thrashed the water with his hands. "Get in here already." Emma and I looked at each other and, after a few seconds of hesitation, turned and ran for the water.

We must have looked like complete lunatics as the three of us began splashing each other with water while cheering at the top of our lungs. There weren't too many people on our part of the beach, so it wasn't as if we were disturbing anybody. A couple of German Shepherds walking by decided to join in for a few moments of pleasure, but their owner soon called them away.

When we did finally decide to get out of the water, the sun had dropped low enough to the horizon to ensure the temperature dropped significantly. By the time we returned to the house, the three of us were shivering so badly that Kay thought we might catch pneumonia. Thankfully, the house had two bathrooms, and while Ollie and I jumped into the downstairs one, Emma used the one in Kay and Roger's ensuite.

We must have stood under the hot stream of water for ages because when we finally emerged from the bathroom, dinner had already been set out on the dining room table. To say that the fish and chips were delicious is an understatement, but what I remember most was the cheer that seemed to hang in the air as we shared our brief little adventure with Kay and Roger. They laughed just as hard as we did, and it wasn't just some silly laugh to try and make us feel better. When I told them about the moment Ollie ran between Emma and me and then continued on straight into the water, I could see tears streaming down Kay's face.

With the house only having two bedrooms, the three of us shared the downstairs one. It had a set of bunks against one wall and a couch on the other, and in the middle of the room, this rug that we used to play Monopoly on. Actually, not just Monopoly, but plenty of other board games and card games as well. It's just that Monopoly was the one that kept us the busiest, some games often stretching well close to midnight. A couple of times, we set the game up at the kitchen table so Kay and Roger could join in as well, but the truth is, I think they just enjoyed watching us from a distance, three kids who'd finally found a piece of the world worth living in.

The other game we loved playing was Yahtzee, the one with five dice and a cup. We each took turns to score, and this one time when it was Emma's turn to score, she put my surname behind her name and then Ollie's.

"We're family," she said with a matter-of-fact tone. "And family all have the same last name."

"Yes, they do," Ollie agreed, and after clapping Emma on the back, he grabbed the cup and began to roll.

I didn't tell them how much that meant to me, but the truth is, it was one of those moments that forever stood out to me, such a little token that brought us ever so closer together. Games were what brought us together, but it was the little things that made them so special.

When we woke up a couple of mornings after our arrival and made our way into the kitchen, Kay had already made breakfast for everybody, a mix of scrambled eggs, bacon, toast, cereal, and fruit waiting for us. Roger had already left to go for a round of golf with his brother-in-law. Kay had planned to go shopping with her sister, Judith, and she gave us a choice to go with them or spend some alone time exploring the town. Of course, we opted for the latter, the three of us not even needing to vote.

When we walked out of the house just after ten, I don't think you could have found three happier people in all of England, perhaps even the world. Kay had also given me a twenty-pound note as I said bye to her and told me to make sure I shared my wealth with the rest of my friends, a request I promised to keep. So, with our bellies full, money in our pockets, and the sun shining down from above, we headed out to make memories, memories we knew we would carry for a lifetime.

Actually, that last part is complete bullshit. Whoever tells you that they know they're about to have the kinds of adventures you'll yearn for in the future is either a fantasist or a liar. Imagine the days we'd have as kids if we only knew that those days would be some of the best of our lives. We'd make every single minute of every single hour of every single day count, and I doubt we'd be able to enjoy any of them. What makes those moments so special is when they pop up again in your memories in years to come, and usually when you're trapped in a place darker than you ever imagined possible. It's only *because* of that darkness that the light really shines, isn't it?

The first place we headed to was the same place where we had such riotous fun that first evening, the place where Ollie decided to dunk himself in the ocean fully clothed. This time, when we approached the pebbled beach, he resisted the temptation to repeat the act and simply pretended to start running before stopping when he got the laughs from Em and me.

We slowly walked along the foreshore and took in the atmosphere of the place. Colourful buildings lined the roadway fronting the beach, and people filled the street while inspecting the wares of multiple stalls in what appeared to be some sort of market.

"Is that fairy floss I see?" Ollie asked when he pointed to one stall in particular and immediately began jumping up and down on the spot. "Oh, please, Father dearest, could you spare some loose change for the kiddies so they might eat this wondrous concoction?" Emma began to giggle as I looked at him with a dumb expression on my face.

"Huh?"

"Geez, Jack," Ollie said as he switched voices to one of his many characters. "You're the man with the money, the moola,...zee dabloons," he said while holding a hand out and rubbing his thumb across the fingers.

"Oh, of course," I said, finally catching up. "OK, let's get some fairy floss."

It turned out that no kid could ever be content with just a wand of fairy floss at a market. An hour later, we were buzzing from the ultimate sugar rush courtesy of three generously-sized bottles of Lime pop from one stall, a bunch of chocolate variations from another, and some candied almonds that I instantly grew addicted to from another. Emma also grabbed herself some freshly made licorice that

Ollie pretended to barf from. To make matters worse, Em would also chew a piece and then pretend to let the thick black drool run down her chin before displaying black-stained teeth when she grinned.

One of the stalls we did all stop to take a look at was the one where this old guy was selling homemade kites, the designs some of the craziest I'd ever seen. He'd printed a few famous characters onto some, as well as original designs onto others, designs that included space themes, fairytales, and war machines. Some of them looked so realistic. I suggested that we each get one to take them further down the beach to fly, and everybody agreed. I immediately went for the dragon, its tail stretching some three or four metres behind it. Ollie chose a dinosaur, while Emma chose something called Sailor Moon. She told me it was from a Japanese cartoon, but I'd never heard of it before. She seemed really drawn to it, and so I didn't mind paying the extra two pounds it cost over the price of my own.

Halfway down the beach, Ollie became impatient and started pretending to fly his kite while we walked along the water's edge. When the breeze suddenly kicked up and pulled the pterodactyl free from his hands, it suddenly soared into the sky, the spool of string ripped from his hands. He shouted in panic and began chasing it as Em and I watched to see if he'd manage to reel it back in.

Catch it he did, but not before the great creature flew to nearly the entire length of string available to it. We had to tilt our heads up physically to keep sight of it before Ollie finally brought it back down to earth. Once he knew he had it safely secured again, the cheering began, sending me and Emma into renewed hysterics.

We flew the kites for most of the day, the wind giving us the perfect amount of lift without sucking the life out of our new-found craft. I don't think any of them ever looked quite as cool as what Ollie's did during that maiden flight, but they came close, especially my dragon. The body just felt a little disproportionate to the rest of the beast, whereas Ollie's appeared exactly as you'd imagine the flying dinosaur would have looked.

To me, that was the day that started our friendship for real, a bond that I would never again find in my entire life. The three of us were more than just friends or even siblings if we'd been lucky enough to have been placed into the same home. I don't exactly know the right term to use. If we had been lovers, then perhaps soulmate might have been appropriate, but our connection went deeper than that, deeper than the closest love affair imaginable. We were survivors... survivors of a struggle few could ever truly understand.

13

W hen we got back to London a week later, Ollie had to go to Wales with his aunt for a couple of weeks due to a family emergency. It meant that when school restarted, it was just Emma and me who ended up going. It felt strange not to have him around, and most lunchtimes, we would just sit out in the playground, eating our lunch in silence, some days not speaking a word the entire time. It wasn't that we no longer liked each other. It was quite the opposite, in fact. We valued each other more than anything. It was just that we'd grown so close that words weren't always needed. With Ollie gone, it felt like an integral link in our chain had been taken, and what was left was just dangling in the breeze, waiting for that reconnection.

Ollie's absence ended up stretching out to five weeks. He missed nearly half the semester, which is not a good thing for someone already struggling to keep up. His dyslexia proved quite a challenge for him, even with all the extra help he was getting. I know that his teacher wasn't thrilled by him missing such a large chunk, and she did try to organize for work to be sent to him, but it never eventuated due to his mother neglecting to answer messages.

I sometimes wonder just how far back I'd have to go to find the single event that eventually led us to where fate had ultimately planned for us to end up. For Ollie, it might have been those five weeks away from school, five weeks spent away from friends who could have supported him during a time of stress and confusion.

What we didn't know at the time was that Ollie's guardian wasn't just some random angel who opened their heart and their home the way Roger and Kay did with me. In fact, Ollie rarely spoke about his home life at all, something Emma and I never questioned since we both understood how deep some of the associated emotions could reach. It was his deceased mother's best friend who took him in seven years after her death, and seven years after watching him dumped at a nearby orphanage. By the time she decided to take him in, he'd all but forgotten about his family, and she was just another stranger to him.

The emergency that kept Ollie from school for all those weeks was his guardian's mother passing away from suicide. She'd phoned her daughter moments before throwing herself off a cliff, and because authorities had failed to find a body, there were a lot of loose ends needing tying up, including a sizable estate her three children were already frothing at the mouth over.

When Ollie did eventually return, we saw the difference in him immediately. He'd grown even skinnier than ever, his skin blemished from all the stress and anxiety. His hair had grown long, the tangled mass a far cry from the well-groomed style he had during our holiday. The worst part was that he'd also begun smoking cigarettes. He offered us one during our first lunchtime together, and both Emma and I declined.

He wasn't angry, per se, but we could see the emotions running rampant within him. I would have called it frustration more than anything; the scars in his soul reopened once more.

"Aunt Vicky thinks she's going to get at least six-hundred thousand quid when her mother's estate is finally sold," he told us while smoking his second cigarette in a row. "She promised for us to buy a bigger house and go on a holiday to America." He looked at each of us in turn. "I'll make sure you guys come with us."

"We'd need passports," Emma said. "Not easy to get."

"We'll get them. Money can get you anything," Ollie said with a grin that gave me chills.

Late one Friday afternoon, less than three weeks later, Ollie met me in the same park where we first met, and while sitting against the same tree that Emma had been using that fateful day, Ollie pulled out a pack of cigarettes. He casually pulled one out as he began to explain how his aunt was completely losing the plot due to the delay of the estate not being sold.

"There's still no body," he told me as he flicked the lighter a couple of times until it lit and then chased the tip of the cigarette with the flame until the end of it finally caught. "And unless a judge is willing to declare her dead, this could stretch out for years."

It wasn't until the smell hit me that I first noticed the shape of the cigarette. It had no filter and looked like it had been rolled using a gravel road for support. It was marijuana, the joint hanging out from between his lips as he gazed off to the roadway. I'm not sure whether I was surprised or shocked, but the sight of that cigarette definitely made me uncomfortable.

"Olli, why, man?"

"Why what?" I pointed to the cigarette and frowned. "It's just dope. Don't fret."

He instantly became defensive, and when I knocked back his offer to take a puff, he shook his head in disgust.

"I thought we were friends."

"We are," I snapped. "Why would that change just because I don't want to take a stupid drag?"

"You would if Em was here." He began to sound obnoxious, and it was starting to irritate me.

"What?"

"Oh, go on, don't deny it." He tried to dig his elbow into my side, but I shoved his arm aside.

"I don't know what you're talking about," I said and tried to change the subject. "I'm sure a judge will do what needs to be done."

"You like her, don't you?"

"Of course I do. You do, too."

"Yeah, but not like that."

"What?"

"You got the hots for her," Ollie said. "Just admit it already." I could see the aggravation in his eyes. He wanted a fight, and he wasn't going to stop until he got one.

I had a choice to make, and neither option felt particularly appealing. The first was to stay and try to talk him down again, to see if I could make him see sense. I didn't know how long he'd been on drugs for, nor how long he'd been smoking the dope for that day, but what I did know was they were already affecting him in a way that wasn't going to help him.

My second option was to walk away, just get up and let him be. I could ignore his insults and brush them aside the way Melvin had shown me, go back home, and pretend like this conversation had never taken place. What I didn't think was that Ollie was going to like that much, not the way his eyes kept zeroing in on me with those narrow slits. He looked like a predator hunting for its next meal, and I appeared to be on the menu.

"You're not thinking straight," I finally said and figuring Option 2 would be the wiser one to go with, I pushed myself off the ground and began to walk away. Just as I knew he would, Ollie continued throwing insults at me, hoping for one of them to trigger me enough to blow up at him.

"Yeah, run away, Jack. Because that's what you're good at. Don't bother facing up to the truth...JUST RUN AWAY."

A couple of kids kicking a football between each other stopped to look, no doubt waiting for something more physical to happen, but Ollie remained where he sat, and I didn't bother stopping. Sometimes, it's just better to walk away, and that's exactly what I did. He eventually stopped throwing the insults, and I could feel his gaze in the back of my head, but I continued on regardless.

That weekend was one of the longest as I waited to see whether Ollie would make the first move. I assumed he was embarrassed by the whole thing and would come around and apologize, but he never did. Emma came to see me on the Sunday afternoon, and we played a bit of Nintendo while talking about everything else except Ollie. I don't know whether it was because I was trying to avoid telling her why we fought in the first place or because I didn't want to sound like *that guy* who's too straight-laced. In fact, we spent almost three hours together before Em finally mentioned something about him.

"I'm worried about him, Jack," she said once we decided to switch off the console. "I heard that his aunt has been drinking a lot, and you know how vulnerable he is. She got herself kicked out of the Pint and Pickle a couple of nights ago, and Marcy Jones told me that he went down there in a fit of rage and tried to hit the bartender."

"He did?" The news surprised me, but then I remembered the joint and wondered how much of that anger came from the drugs.

"He's smoking dope," I told her and proceeded to tell her about the fight...*all* of the fight, including the incriminating part about me. Emma listened until I finished, and while I expected her to point out the part about me supposedly liking her, she skipped it entirely.

"We have to help him," she said. "I don't know how or if it's even possible, but we have to try."

That was when we agreed to go to Ollie's house to see whether helping him was a possibility. I called out to Kay that we were headed out, and she popped her head out of the kitchen with a smudge of flour on her cheek, her signature look when baking.

"Pop a coat on; it's cold out," she said, and I promised I would.

We walked the dozen blocks to Ollie's house mostly in silence, the sky eerily dark as the weather threatened to turn on us. Kay had been right about the cold, the wind biting hard each time it kicked up into our faces. Emma didn't have a coat, and I could see her trying to keep warm by wrapping her arms tight around herself, so I did what any guy with a shred of decency would.

"Here, take this," I said as I pulled the jacket off.

"No, I'm -"

"Just take it," I said, half-flinging it over her shoulders before she gave in and slipped her arms into it.

When we reached Ollie's house just before six, it looked as if someone had taken a rage to the home. The front yard had broken plates and glasses littered across it, with what looked like the broken remnants of a microwave oven.

"What the hell happened here?" I whispered as we made our way to the front door.

"Aunt Vicky is cleaning out all the crap she doesn't need anymore," a voice suddenly said and we looked over to see Ollie sitting amongst a couple of the overgrown bushes in the garden bed.

For a second, I couldn't tell whether he had decided to start using makeup or was wearing some strange kind of mask, but then Emma's reaction made it clear what I was seeing.

"Ollie, what happened?" she asked as she made a dash for him. I cringed as she almost stepped on a dangerous-looking glass shard sticking up out of the ground, but she missed by mere inches.

"Fell down the stairs," he mused as he drew on his cigarette, and when he exhaled with a huge grin, I saw one of his front teeth was missing. "Or was it walking into a door?"

He began to giggle hysterically as Em and I exchanged a look. With no smell of alcohol coming off him, we assumed it was because of the other vice now in his life.

"Ollie, please," Em whispered as she knelt down beside him. The laughter continued for a few moments longer before he finally reined it back in again.

"Sorry, maybe it's not so funny," he mumbled to himself and took another drag.

"We're here for you, you know that," she continued. "You can always come and stay with me if you want to. Just until you get things sorted out here."

I remained back, knowing when to keep quiet and let those in a better position do the talking. Ollie did steal a couple of glances in my direction, and I could tell he still had issues with me.

"How would your boyfriend feel about that?"

"He's not my boyfriend," Emma snapped, and when she slapped his chest, Ollie looked at her wide-eyed. "And don't you dare use that as an excuse so you can act like a dick. We're all hurting, all of us. What gives you the right to try and use us to ease your own?"

She was pissed, and not just a little bit. For a few seconds, they just stared at each other as if I didn't exist at all. Ollie looked like he'd been slapped in the face for the first time in his life, unable to comprehend the sensation and unsure of how to proceed. Fortunately for him, Emma did.

"Now get up, shake hands with Jack and come home with me." As if to double down on her order, she stood, folded her arms across her chest and stared down at him.

Ollie looked from her to me and back again, perhaps weighing up whether she was serious or not. The cigarette he'd been using as distraction had burnt down to just a stub, and when he finally realized that she was serious, he flicked it away and held a hand up to me.

"Help an old man up, would you, son?"

His humour returning was a good sign, although it was still far from the apology we would need to ease the tension between us. When I held out a hand for him and pulled him to his feet, he didn't let go once he was upright. He kind of held it before using his other hand to pat the one he was already holding.

"I'm sorry for being a dick to you, man."

"Forget about it," I said, feeling the heat rise in my cheeks at the unexpected apology.

When he finally let go of my hand, Emma came and stood next to him before throwing an arm around each of our shoulders. Ollie threw his opposite arm around mine, and I did likewise with Emma as we stood in a tight little circle, the three of us back together. What I didn't know at the time was that that was one of those moments I would look back on with the kind of heaviness that brought tears, wishing that I had taken the time to truly savour the moment. If I had, then maybe the events from the following days wouldn't have been so painful.

14

When I walked home alone that early Sunday evening back in the Autumn of '99, after watching Ollie and Emma head off in the opposite direction, I tried to picture each of our futures, the possible lives each of us would eventually lead. For Ollie, who struggled with school work and now clearly had addiction issues already at the ripe old age of thirteen, I figured he'd end up as some sort of tradesman, perhaps a mechanic even. He had this genuine passion for cars and motorbikes. I'd seen him working on his aunt's lawn-mower once, brining the broken piece of crap to life with just a couple of cheap replacement parts.

Emma, on the other hand, I imagined as some sort of counsellor. She had that kind of genuine empathy that seemed to draw people in, this ability to connect with people on a much deeper level. I called it soul whispering and had experienced it myself more than a few times. She could see inside a person's mind and understand problems on a completely different level than most people. I figured that if she managed to get her schooling right, she might even end up as a psychologist or psychiatrist.

For me, I couldn't even take a guess at my future, let alone make predictions about the kind of job I might have. I wasn't exactly flunking school and managed to get pretty decent grades when I really put my mind to it. My issue was that I could get distracted at the drop of a hat, especially when it came to my friends. I cared about them and often spent a lot of time thinking about their problems.

At the time, I had grown so fond of watching the planes fly over our house that I sometimes pictured myself at the controls of one of those beasts. A pilot flying a huge jumbo was the kind of dream a kid could get used to. I once asked one of my teachers what sort of grades someone needed to become an airline pilot, and Mr. Henderson at first grinned at me and then broke into laughter, turning my face bright red as a few of the other kids in the class joined in.

There were two types of teachers I came to recognize during my school years. The kind who liked kids, and the kind who didn't. Henderson was the latter, often getting his kicks by keeping students back after school for the dumbest of things. He also frequently volunteered to be the supervising teacher during lunchtime detention, a position he filled more than any other at our school.

"I wouldn't be setting the bar quite so high for yourself, Hardy," was the advice he ended up leaving me with that day, and I sometimes wish I had used it to my advantage instead of discounting it and walking away in a pissed-off mood. Perhaps that was my pivotal moment in life where I could have used that embarrassed feeling to drive me forward, proving him wrong. I sometimes now look back at that moment and picture myself years later walking through some airport terminal in my pilot's uniform and running into that teacher. Oh, the things I could have said to him, milking that delicious feeling of success for all it was worth.

By the time I reached home, day had already turned into night, and when I reached the front fence of our home, I stopped when I saw Roger and Kay through the living room window. They were standing in the archway leading into the kitchen, the curtains not yet drawn, and giving me the perfect view of the place. They were holding each other, their arms wrapped around their middle, with Kay's head tilted against the crook of Roger's neck. He must have said something to her because she suddenly looked up at him with a smile and then closed her eyes when he leaned down and kissed her.

I remained standing there for a few minutes, not wanting to dare interrupt their moment together. The truth is, it was their love that I often hoped I would find for myself one day. I had never seen that type of love before moving in with them, a pure kind of connection that just seemed perfect. The kiss only lasted a second or two, but they held each other for a lot longer as they began to dance slowly on the spot. I think that was the moment I really felt the love between them and hoped it would last forever.

Just as I was about to sit on the fence and wait out their moment, Kay suddenly looked over her shoulder and pulled free as something in the kitchen drew her attention. Roger let her go and leaned against the archway, watching her. I'm guessing it had been something on the stove because when I finally managed to walk inside, the smell of the dinner she was busy making filled the air.

"Ah, look who made it just in time," Roger quipped when he saw me walk in. "Perfect timing, kiddo."

"It smells good," I said and walked into the kitchen and waved at Kay.

"Well, you're in for a treat because Mrs. Preston doesn't make her famous corned brisket often, but when she does..." He rolled his eyes in delight and ran his tongue over his lips.

"Oh, quit it," Kay said as she waved his words away with an embarrassed grin. "It's nothing special."

How wrong she was. That meal tasted almost as perfect as the vision I had seen waiting to walk into the house that evening, the flavours some of the most intense ever. Most dishes only had one or two elements that made them so delicious, but this one seemed to have it all, each individual item its own little morsel of perfection. Yes, I like to go on about food. It's one of the few things I can understand consistently in my life. It's also one of those strange sensations that manages to follow us through the years like little time capsules, pockets of emotions linked to taste. If I close my eyes now and think back to that night, I can still feel the tingling as the vinegar from the meat mixed with the white sauce hit my tongue.

We didn't always sit at the dining room table to eat our meals. Occasionally, Kay would insist on us taking our plates into the living room and grabbing one of the folding tables to rest them on as she put on some funny show to make us laugh. Seinfeld was her favourite, although she did put on the occasional episode of Friends as well. Roger said it was because she had a thing for Matt Le Blanc, which always made her blush profusely.

That night wasn't one of the nights we went to the living room; instead, we remained at the dining table as Roger shared the details of his latest book. He spoke with such passion as he explained the plot behind his latest protagonist, a hitman named Theodore Deville, who spoke with a deep French accent despite being Irish. It was while talking us through his first contract killing that he paused mid-sentence, the break enough to pull my attention up off my plate.

His fork sat midway between his mouth and the plate, his eyes fixed directly across the table as he seemed frozen in place. The moment only lasted a second, but it felt like an eternity. When he spoke his wife's name, I followed his gaze, and what I saw made me drop my fork, the bang of it hitting the edge of the plate perhaps the signal he needed to break his paralysis.

The moment I saw her, I knew something was wrong. Kay still looked across the table at her husband, but her eyes lacked the focus a person recognized as attention. One after the other, they began to roll slowly into the back of their sockets, the left one briefly twitching before it disappeared. Too stunned to move, I watched as Roger first screamed his wife's name and then made a mad dash to get to her when she began to slide sideways off her chair.

I don't remember Roger screaming for me to call an ambulance, but I know I did because I remember briefly forgetting our address when the operator asked for it. Panic is a funny thing, able to make shit moments even worse. The ambulance eventually showed up, and I led them inside while Roger continued talking to his wife. I don't know if she had lost consciousness by then, but she wasn't awake when I saw her being wheeled out on the stretcher.

The next couple of hours went by like a blur as images of Roger and me racing to the hospital blended in with the run through the hallways followed by us sitting in this brightly-lit waiting room all alone. Roger never spoke to me, his anxiety at maximum as he continuously paced back and forth from one door to the other. All I could do was sit there in silence, watching him go through what felt like the worst moment of his life.

There was this one moment, this infinitesimal point in time where I did happen to catch Roger look in my direction, a sideways glance that came when he reached the far end of the room and turned around to restart the trip back. Our eyes met for just a speck of a second, but what I saw in those eyes frightened me more than the previous two hours. What I saw was annoyance, not at the situation, not because of the lack of information coming from the doctors and nurses, and not even because of the unbearable torture of being forced to wait.

No, the annoyance was because I was there. My presence alone was what annoyed him, and once I saw that look and understood it, I knew that my life was headed down a completely different path to the one I thought I was on just a few hours before while watching my adopted parents embracing their love. In the blink of an eye, the illusion that had drawn me in and kept me fooled for months had finally faltered, letting in a brief glimpse of reality, the kind I had been running from all along.

When the news finally came, the doctor delivering it first asked Roger to sit down and, when he refused, insisted on it. A nurse had also entered the room, and I think it was her job to keep me busy while the news was being delivered, although she only stood some distance away watching the doctor and Roger. That was another moment where I felt like a real imposter.

It was a stroke, and a significant one at that. The doctors had to drill a hole into Kay's head to relieve the pressure from the bleeding, and while I couldn't make out most of what was being said, I did hear the doctor warn Roger to prepare himself for the worst. I remember wondering what it must have felt like to tell a man that the love of his life was on the brink of death and there was nothing anybody could do for her.

Roger didn't cry, not then, at least. Instead, he sat in that chair and just stared at the floor with a vacant expression. Both the doctor and nurse stayed for a few moments but eventually left the two of us alone again. I don't know whether Roger even remembered that I was there because he sat like that for exactly two hours and forty minutes, according to the clock on the wall. I know because I wondered whether he would ever move again.

The crying came when he finally stood and walked to the window, where he stopped and pressed both hands against the glass. I'd been debating whether to ask him about the location of a toilet as my bladder had been pressing my insides for the better part of an hour, and I wasn't about to lose control in the middle of that moment.

That sound of him finally losing control still haunts me to this day. I hadn't seen Roger cry before, and when he pressed his face against the glass as if hiding it from me, he finally let the pain out. The sobbing sounded angry, as if his soul had been betrayed by fate itself, and he wanted to call it out for its brutal deception. Unable to move, I had to sit in that seat and watch a man whom I had respected and grown to look up to collapse to the ground as he felt his world crumble before his eyes. I knew Kay was his everything, and without her in his life, I doubted that we had any chance of continuing together.

For three days, Kay languished on the very precipice of death, the doctors giving her just a five-percent chance of survival. Roger never left her side once he was allowed in to see her, and after that first day, it was arranged for me to stay with Emma until whatever was happening with Kay would be finalized.

I don't know whether it was hope or just that hidden dread of going back to my old life, but something kept me from even considering returning to Whispering Hall. I kept envisioning Kay coming home and spending weeks in bed recovering, Roger bringing in a nurse to help out with her. I even pictured myself making breakfast some mornings and bringing it to Kay on a tray. Sadly, those visions never came to pass.

When the news finally came, it didn't take long for the dream I had been living to come crashing down around me. Kay didn't die, but she did face months, perhaps years, of ongoing therapy. She also wouldn't be coming back home for what the doctor described as a significant amount of time. Instead, she would be transferred to a care facility. Her left side remained completely paralyzed, her speech completely unintelligible. Or that's what I heard, at least.

You see, I never saw Kay again, not after catching a brief glimpse of her lying in that hospital bed before I was ushered out of the room. The last image I have of Kay was her looking at my direction with shame in her eyes. I don't know whether she felt guilty for failing me, but that's what I saw in her eyes. I wish I could have run to her, told her that she hadn't failed anybody, but I never got the chance.

I stayed with Emma and her family for two weeks before the knock on the door I had been dreading finally came. Alison Farrow had already been to my house and collected a bag Roger had packed for me. If you think it's harsh getting pushed away like that, then you have finally understood what it's really like to be a victim of the system. The coldness never leaves you, and the constant fear of loneliness is never far from your mind. It's one of the reasons why Ollie, Emma, and I became so close. We knew what friendship meant because, for us, it was so much more than that. To me, they were my real family.

15

As you might have guessed, I ended up back at Whispering Hall, this time a little older and perhaps a little wiser, but definitely a lot more mentally prepared. Actually, no, not just mentally prepared. I think I came back with a shield twice the size of the one I'd left with, which I could use to protect myself. I barely noticed the welcoming committee upon my return and ignored most of the insults thrown by a few of the boys.

My first night back was probably also the toughest, with sleep the furthest thing from my mind. Do you remember how I said that the best times of your life only really appear as such during the darkest moments? Well, this was one of those moments where I couldn't help but think about that summer down in Bexhill with my friends, the three of us laughing and enjoying the challenge of keeping those kites aloft.

I lay in that bunk on my back, staring up into the memories of my past as I watched Ollie run between Emma and me on his way to the water. I watched Emma try that first piece of licorice and then close her eyes in delight as she immediately felt the wave of sweetness rush through her. Most of all, I remembered the three of us sitting on a nearby pier with our feet dangling over the edge, watching the sun set over the town. We told each other secrets that day, the kind we promised to keep forever.

I think there comes a point in every kid's life where they realize that their childhood had been nothing but a great big lie, told to them by grown-ups for whatever reason. That night was the first time I felt like my own childhood had vanished in the blink of an eye, replaced by the man I would eventually become. My voice hadn't quite broken, and the...*other* changes that come with puberty hadn't quite taken a hold, but what change I did notice was that my thinking became a lot more protective.

From that night onward, I began to think less about getting the chance to play the gaming consoles and more about my next meal. I started thinking about new ways I might try to get out completely, to maybe find a job. I wasn't far from turning fourteen, and I'd heard kids getting proper paying jobs at fourteen. Why not me? All I needed was to find someone willing to give me a go.

The other change I noticed wasn't so much a change, but rather a new kind of emotional challenge. When you live in a place like Whispering Hall, you tend to quickly learn that resources are limited and, sometimes, the laws of the jungle take over. You know the ones, like only the strong survive. One of those resources which always seemed to run out was food. There just never seemed to be enough to go around, or at least not enough to fill that dark hole of hunger that was never quite satisfied. As it turned out, it was the very following night that I discovered a new kind of satisfaction.

Meatloaf is what we were served on my second night back. I remember it clearly because, for one, I hated the taste of the meatloaf because of a particular spice I couldn't identify, but more so, because once the meal was finished, I was still just as hungry as when it began. Like I said, there just wasn't enough to go around, and unlike some of the other bigger boys, I tended to hold back so some of the younger ones could get a bit more onto their plates.

The one thing I had never done before was to sneak back into the kitchen well after mealtime to go looking for some food. Stealing within Whispering Hall carried with it severe punishment if caught, but given the way I felt, I didn't care. I needed something to silence the continuing rumbling in my stomach and didn't really care what. And while I did eventually find some, it wasn't the food that satisfied me.

What I found was some left-over mashed potatoes. Not exactly a prized meal, so to speak, but with a little tomato sauce, it was good to go. I ate it crouched beside the fridge, the part of the kitchen where the main bench shielded me from anybody walking past the door. I could still see out because of the low angle from where I knelt. The food was OK, and it did hit the spot, but it was the act of getting it that proved the most satisfying.

When you're caught in a world filled with predators, it's hard to navigate through the jungle and come out the other side unscathed. The deepest scars I bore were those running across my soul, the damage coming from multiple different sources that weren't always physical. When I stole that small, insignificant pile of food, some-thing...almost...primal came over me.

I felt what I can only describe as control, for a brief moment in time, owning something that I desperately needed and had to hang onto. The way my eyes darted towards any noise that might indicate a threat like some desperate predator, or how I ate the food with speed to make it disappear before someone else could snatch it away from me again. I felt...alive, in a way, awake to the fact that for once in my life, I had taken control of my destiny, and nobody could take it from me.

Over the coming weeks and months, I often ventured into the kitchen to steal food, sometimes when I wasn't hungry at all. It was the thrill of it that I needed to feel, the danger somehow the part that kept me wanting. At times, I would even take some random bit of food that I brought back to my bed, if only just to hold something of value that I could hold as my own. We're talking about completely insignificant food, like a slice of bread or a piece of fruit. It was the meaning behind it that mattered, that emotional ownership over something.

The kitchen wasn't the only place I went to steal things from, either. There was this foster home I ended up going to a couple of months after returning to Whispering Hall, where life took a turn for the worst. It turned out that when you reached a certain age in the system, it didn't regard you as much of a priority case anymore, and so they would randomly move you around if someone else needed your spot at the current allocation. Whispering Hall was seen as one of the better facilities, and I guess a more vulnerable kid needed my bed.

I ended up getting moved to the Buxton's Home for Boys in early 2000, and from the moment I arrived, my life went to shit. The beatings became a daily occurrence, not just from other boys but also from two of the carers employed to watch us. Henry Franklin even made it a point to come to your room if he had the urge to dish out some punishment, his choice of weapon being his belt. He'd swing that thing like a cowboy, the buckle leaving grapefruit-sized bruises wherever it connected. A lot of the boys made it a point to avoid him like the plague, especially on a Friday night when he'd be drinking.

The rooms we slept in were set out like a prison, or so some of the others said. I'd never seen the inside of one, so I couldn't be sure if they were just trying to pull a swift one. Two boys to a room and a dozen rooms per floor, three floors in all. At night, one of the duty staff would conduct rounds every hour, and it was in between these rounds that some of the boys went walking.

While the popular place to go to was the area behind the laundry room, a small building attached to the main one, where it was common to find kids smoking, drinking, or popping whatever pills someone had smuggled in, I always wound up going to the kitchen. I still had that primal urge for the hunt, followed by the need to hide and keep safe whatever I had managed to score.

It was during one of those nightly trips that I happened to find one of the offices down the main corridor open, the door usually locked like all the rest. But that night, someone had been inside it, left the light on, and hadn't bothered to close it up again, so an inquisitive kid like me wanted to check it out. I had no intention of stealing anything; it was more just a curiosity.

The office had just a single desk in it, with a computer monitor and a phone on it. When I sat down on the chair, I pretended that it was my desk and I was the one in charge. OK, so it might have been another one of those childish imagination kind of things, but it's what I thought about. Anything was better than the truth.

The keyboard and mouse sat on the movable keyboard tray, and seeing it, I thought I'd continue the illusion by pretending to type something. I pulled out the tray, and that was when it happened. The computer must have just been hibernating because the second the mouse moved ever so slightly, the screen suddenly flickered to life as a fan spun to life inside the computer case. At first, just the Windows logo appeared, but after a few moments, it disappeared, and a webpage opened up, revealing what the previous person had been looking at.

"What the hell are you doing, kid?" a voice suddenly called out, and I looked up to see Henry Franklin standing in the doorway.

I'm pretty sure that if I hadn't seen what I did on the screen, the thrashing would have still been the same. I mean, the guy lived for beating up kids. It was his MO in life, if you know what I mean. But I did see the screen, and Franklin knew I had, which was why he exploded in an instant.

Despite carrying enough extra weight to keep him powered for years without food, he moved with the grace of an Olympic sprinter. He ripped the belt from his pants halfway across the office, and the buckle slammed into my upper left arm with vengeance. White heat exploded as I tried to flinch back, but the buckle hit me a second time, and then a third. I tried to cry out, but the air in my lungs felt locked in place.

When his feet finally carried him close enough for his hands to reach me, Franklin began launching one punch after another. He stole a quick glance at the screen to confirm his suspicions and seeing the gay porn site only further exasperated his rage. My arms and legs copped the brunt of the attack as I managed to mostly shield my face, but a couple of lucky punches also managed to break through. Blood soon began to flow from cuts to my lips and eyebrows.

Franklin outmatched me in every category, much faster and stronger than me by a long way. But what I had that he could never understand was that deep-seated survival instinct, and when you feel your survival being threatened, anything goes. I don't remember my hand ever searching for it, but I suddenly found my fingers wrapped around something solid. Instinct closed my fingers around it tighter, and it was that will to survive that made me raise the phone and slam it into the side of my attacker's face. The sound of it connecting with his head echoed from the corners of the room as he stumbled back a step or two. His attack briefly paused as he tried to comprehend what had just happened.

"Why, you little -" he began, but I didn't wait for him to finish. I threw the phone directly into his face and then jumped from the chair. I made it just three steps towards the door when one of his meaty hands grabbed my arm. "I'm gonna make you wish - " was as far as he got before I did what I had never thought possible. I swung a balled-up fist at him that slammed into the middle of his face, the crunch of his nose breaking sounding more satisfying than the phone.

I had never seen a tomato punch before, but that is the only way I can describe it. Blood ejected from both sides of his nose as my fist connected with him like a hammer. Franklin cried out in utter disbelief, stumbled back a second time and grabbed his face. Not wanting to stick around for Round 3, I sprinted from the office, raced down the hallway and out the front door. Nothing was going to keep me in that house, not even the threat of freezing to death in a snowstorm.

Despite it being the middle of the night at the end of January, I barely felt the cold for the first dozen blocks or so. I ran on pure adrenaline, and when that ran out, I used the anger to fuel my legs. Most of the bleeding had stopped by then, I think because of the extreme cold freezing the wounds shut. When I did eventually slow down to gather my thoughts and realized the possibility of getting hypothermia was real, I began searching for possible ways to keep myself warm.

The answer came to me just a few more blocks down the road

when I found a Salvation Army charity donation bin in front of some shops. After making sure nobody was watching, I managed to climb into the thing and began to try feeling my way through the contents. It wasn't exactly pitch black in there if I half-stood so that my head would keep the door open, but it was still too dark for me to make out the individual items.

I ended up finding a couple of jumpers, a jacket, and a thin blanket that was just big enough for me to wrap myself in. When I heard an approaching siren grow louder, I froze, half expecting the cops to show up, drag me from the bin and take me back to Buxton's Home. I held my breath and waited, listening to the siren first grow higher in pitch as it got closer and then slowly drop off again as it continued on up the road. Only when it faded out completely did I continue dressing myself in whatever clothing I found.

Once I was sure I wasn't going to freeze to death from exposure, I had to find a way to keep myself warm. Even with all the clothes on, as well as the blanket wound around me, the outside temperature continued tormenting me inside my makeshift hideaway. I found that if I could somehow keep moving, I could generate enough body heat to keep me somewhat comfortable.

Fighting through the pain caused by my earlier beating, I began shadow boxing as I sat with my feet pressed against the opposing wall. It wasn't easy, but it did keep the blood circulating fast enough to build up some heat. I also began to hum to give myself some rhythm, and I don't laugh, but I found that Staying Alive by the Bee Gees had the best tempo. The problem was that my energy wasn't unlimited, and soon, I began to slow down.

There came a moment during the night where I wanted to do nothing but fall asleep, my eyeballs close to rolling out of my head. I'd almost resolved myself to a fate somewhere between freezing to death and asphyxiation from entangling myself between more and more pieces of clothing. That was when I paused to let my arms and legs rest for a bit, and the second I did, the other endlessly working machine began to tick over.

My brain never rested, always working on some problem or

another, more so since my awakening from childhood, but instead of trying to think of a better way for me to keep warm, it instead began to distract me by turning my attention to better days. Both Ollie's and Emma's faces materialized in my head like a couple of guardians watching over me, each smiling with a hint of empathy. It hurt to see them, and I wondered what they would have been doing at that very same moment.

The last I heard, Ollie had been taken from his aunt's house and placed into a separate foster care home while she went back to rehab. I hated that he had to go through that stuff alone and would have given anything to be there for him. Emma, on the other hand, was still with the same family she had been with when I left, although after our last conversation, I got the feeling that the relationship had been strained for some time because of issues between her foster parents.

Just thinking about the two of them was enough to ease my own mind. It's funny how our problems never seem as significant when we compare them to those of others, especially those whom we care about. If Ollie's new home was anywhere near as bad as the one I had just escaped from, then I knew a kid like him would struggle to make it through each day. He already had it tough enough without being bombarded by overzealous guardians and bullies wanting to beat on him.

I don't know how I managed to do it, but the cold didn't kill me that night. Yes, it was about as uncomfortable as you might imagine, and I certainly didn't sleep a wink, but as soon as I noticed daylight begin to creep in through tiny holes in the metal sides, I climbed out of my shelter and took inventory of my situation. Thankfully, the traffic hadn't yet picked up. A taxi did slow down when I first jumped out, but I gave him a wave before he continued on with a shake of the head. I don't think he was in the mood for a chat about homeless people surviving on the streets during winter.

The other reason he might have been staring at me in a weird way was because of the jumper I was wearing; the bright purple reminded me of Barney the Dinosaur. I quickly ripped it off again to reveal a cool black Nike jumper underneath, although it was significantly thinner and immediately let the frigid air in. I did hesitate before tossing it back inside the bin, weighing up looks over warmth.

What I didn't want to do was draw attention to myself. I wasn't sure how Franklin would have followed up his beating of me, but I assumed that at some time, he would have had to report my escape to the relevant authorities who would, in turn, report me missing with the Bobbies. If they had already received the memo about me, then most would be on the lookout for someone matching my description. A bright purple jumper would only draw the kind of attention that would get me nabbed, and I had no intention of making it easier for them.

For the first part of that morning, I got moving again, if only to get my temperature up. While the wind from the previous evening had died down considerably, the temperature remained the same, perhaps just a couple of degrees above freezing. With no real gear to protect me, I had to rely on other ways to keep myself warm.

Saving myself from freezing to death was just the first of several issues I had to deal with. The second was the police themselves. They would no doubt have been given the likely area I would be found in, and if my suspicions were correct, then I was still standing smack back in the middle of that proverbial bullseye. I needed to get out of there and fast. If I didn't, then I might as well have walked to the nearest police station and handed myself in.

Somehow, I ended up on a bus headed south. Fare evasion wasn't an easy issue to deal with, but being peak hour, it gave me the cover I needed, the dozens of people at each stop scrambling to get on enough to keep the driver busy. At first, the nerves almost got the better of me, and I continued walking straight past the bus's open door, but when that familiar feeling of forced control took over, the kind I'd felt each time I stole some food for myself, I made the move. Once I was in, the rest was easy.

While I had found a ride out of the danger zone, what I didn't have was a destination. Winter stretched across the entire country, and it didn't matter where I went; the freezing weather would follow. I rode that first bus until two stops from the very end of the line, climbed out, and immediately jumped aboard another. It had only taken less than an hour, and with plenty of commuters still about, it made the transition so much easier.

That second bus ride lasted a bit longer than the first, but I still wasn't sure I knew where I was going. I considered trying my luck at boarding a train to take me out of London, but the thought stirred a memory, and once Ollie and Em popped into my head, I knew exactly where I needed to go. It should have been the first place I thought of, but with everything else on my mind, I forgave myself for not thinking of my friends.

Seven buses is what I caught to get back to the very park where I first met my friends. I only evaded the fares on the first three, though, thanks to a generous Asian man who spotted me a few pounds when I asked him for some money for food. While I could have risked the other four as well and saved myself the money for more important things, I figured karma might eventually catch up with me, and so I decided to do the right thing.

From a distance, the park looked eerily similar, despite the dirty blanket of snow covering the ground, almost as if every previous shade of green had been bled out. What remained was a half-finished portrait with intricate details missing, most hidden by a change of season. The only difference I could see was that the tree where Emma had been sitting when I first met her was gone. I learned later that a lightning strike had destroyed it during a rather intense thunderstorm a couple of months earlier.

I don't know what made me stay, but a part of me figured that fate would once again intervene and, by some pure miracle, one of my friends would turn up. Of course, I knew it couldn't have been Ollie, unless he'd done a runner like I had, but perhaps Emma would feel some random urge to check out the old park.

Ignoring the snow, I sat down cross-legged on the spot where the tree once stood, patiently waiting for fate to show up. Before long, the melting snow beneath my butt soaked through the jeans I was wearing and when I began shivering, I knew it was time to go. I guess it wouldn't surprise you to know that I ended up going to Emma's house, but after knocking on the door for a good hour, I knew that this time, fate wasn't with me.

Did I ever truly believe that it would be as easy as just showing up at a friend's house and they would save me? Probably not. Maybe I believed that old fairytale myth about a *Happily Ever After* waiting for everybody somewhere in time. Reality is far more brutal. There would be no Happily Ever After for me that day or the ones that came after. What I did do not long after realizing that Emma wasn't going to come and save the day was to walk to a nearby police station and hand myself in. Shortly after I did, I was sitting in a room eating a hotdog, and a short time after that, I was headed home.

16

While I might not have done so well in the Happily Ever After department, I did end up finding myself sent to a new home a month after my fourteenth birthday, one that I found to be just as perfect as Kay and Roger Preston's. This time around, it was a single mother named Rose Chapman who agreed to take me in. Her husband, a former bank manager, had died in a tragic car accident several years earlier and left her a sizable estate, which she used to help underprivileged kids from time to time. She did have a son and two daughters, but all had either grown up and left home or gone off to university, like the youngest girl, Beth, did.

From the moment I arrived, Rose tried her best to make me as comfortable as possible. It felt strange to be in such a different environment, but I knew I could definitely get used to it. I wouldn't have said the woman was overly wealthy, but I could tell that she wasn't exactly short of a quid either. Good-quality furniture filled the home, my room boasting a double bed, television, and a gaming console Rose said had belonged to her son, Ricky. He'd left to join the army and wouldn't be back anytime soon.

I could tell this woman treasured her family. Nearly every wall supported various photo frames displaying the family in various stages of life. Some showed all five members, some others just a couple of the children. A few showed just her husband, and when she pointed them out to me, I detected her voice subtly breaking with emotion.

What I did find odd, though, was that the number of photos showing the kids seemed vastly tilted in favour of just the two daughters. Rose's son, Rick, hardly featured at all, and none showing him in his supposed military uniform, something I would have assumed to be a given. Which parent wouldn't be proud of their child joining the army and affectionately displaying the proof?

I could have asked, I guess, but in the end, I don't think I actually cared much. You have to remember that I hadn't had a very good run with those types of homes, and when I did, something would always happen where the entire experience would turn around and bite me in the arse. I wasn't rude or acted ungrateful. On the contrary. Looking at me from the outside, you would have seen a thrilled kid appearing lost for words most of the time, babbling excitedly about every little thing. Yet on the inside, the picture looked quite different.

I began to use isolation as a way to shield myself. It was easier to avoid being around people altogether. That way, I didn't have to risk getting too close to anybody and forming relationships that would eventually die off anyway. Friends became a thing of the past, except for my current ones, of course. I still made sure to keep in contact with Emma and Ollie as much as I could, although it wasn't always possible. It was during one such call that I found out about Ollie's latest run-in with the law.

Rose wasn't the kind of woman to put up lots of rules around her home, which gave me a new sense of freedom. One of the things I got to use as freely as I wanted was the telephone, and it made contacting Ollie and Em so much easier. I phoned her one night in early April for her birthday. She'd turned fourteen as well, and I remember feeling so bad because I hadn't been able to get her anything. While I had access to practically everything I wanted at my new home, money wasn't one of those things.

"It's OK, Jack, really," she told me after I sang her a Happy Birthday and then proceeded to apologize profusely for being such a lame friend. I genuinely felt bad, and I think she knew that, especially since she understood exactly how it worked in our world. To stop me from going on about it, she subtly changed the topic of conversation. "Have you heard from Ollie lately?"

"No, not for a couple of weeks. Last I heard, he was trying to convince his foster mum to let him get a job with a bricklayer he met. You?"

When I detected a slight pause in her response, I recognized the delay. It was what Emma did whenever she had bad news, the length of the pause usually an indicator of how severe the thing she was about to tell me.

"Ollie got himself arrested," she said with a hint of disappointment.

"What? Are you kidding?"

"I wish I were, but no. It's real. Stole a car with a friend, and they ended up crashing into someone's home after a short police chase."

I closed my eyes when I heard her words, picturing my friend sitting in a stolen car. In my vision, Ollie sat in the passenger seat, egging the driver on as the pair of them passed a joint between each other.

"Oh my God," I finally said as I tried pushing a thumb into my temple.

"Yeah, oh my God is right. He's already in juvie. They remanded him into custody. Who knows what time he'll end up doing."

"I knew the drugs would eventually lead to this," I said, remembering that first time back in the park when I saw him light up a joint. That was when Emma said something surprising.

"It's only dope, Jack. I know he wasn't doing anything harder."

I opened my eyes and stared at the wall in disbelief as her words seemed to echo in my ear. Did I hear right? Did she just defend his drug-taking?

"What do you mean it's only dope, Em? Drugs are drugs."

"Jack, it's a plant, and it's not like anybody actually enforces the law surrounding it." Her words left me in total disbelief.

"People spend serious jail time for it."

"For *selling* it, yes, but not using it."

Her words shocked me, and it took me a few moments to understand something I had never dreamed possible. Once the idea rose up, I found it impossible to shut down again.

"Emma, are you using it as well?"

The question hung between us as the silence closed in around me. I don't think she had expected me to ask, and now that I had, she didn't know how to answer. What I hoped was the truth, the question turning into a test I didn't know I'd set. I think she knew that if she lied at that moment, the broken trust would never be repaired.

"Yes, sometimes."

"You smoke dope?" The words raced out of me before I had a chance to consider them, the revelation hitting me like a ton of bricks. I was totally gobsmacked.

"Jesus, Jack, calm down. I only do it when I'm stressed. It helps calm me down."

"How long?" It was the one question I needed to know above any other, the one question that would reveal just how long there had been secrets between us, secrets I never believed possible.

"Huh?"

"How long have you been smoking dope for?"

"I don't know. A while." The tone she used sounded defensive, but more than that, it sounded dismissive, and that's how I knew that she knew *exactly* how long.

"Em?" That was when she snapped, throwing the answer back at me like an outfielder.

"It was the day I took Ollie home with me, OK?"

I was stunned. We weren't talking days or weeks, but months. *Many* months. Months during which time they kept sneaking around behind my back like a couple of regular junkies.

"Jack?" I barely heard her speak my name as I felt a boat anchor drop into my stomach, the heaviness sinking further with each breath. I felt betrayed and, worse than that, alone. "Jack, are you still there?"

I couldn't answer her. No matter how many times I tried to push a response out, my lips refused to curl around the sound of it, and it just stalled at the back of my throat. When I heard the click of her hanging up the phone and effectively cancelling the connection between us, it felt like a dagger through my heart. Had I really just lost the closest person I had in this world?

That night was one of the worst nights of my life, as I lay in bed unable to close my eyes. With no moon outside and the blinds in my room closed, not even shadows formed on my walls. Pure darkness hung over me, and all I could do was stare into it as I replayed the memory of them walking away from me that long-ago afternoon over and over again. Sometimes, I'd change the truth and call out to them, asking for them to wait up so I could go with them. If I had, then maybe things would have turned out far different from how they had. Maybe I could have talked them out of using drugs altogether, saved the both of them from a future where one of them ends up inside the juvenile justice system at just fourteen. Or maybe, just maybe, I would have ended up joining them.

There were other visions that played out in my head that night, appearing in the darkness above me like some futuristic hologram display. Our history played on repeat, all the events that made our connection so special. In a way, it felt like a goodbye, in some way, a moment for me to look back on the best friends I'd ever had, to help me transition away with that final glimpse.

I must have eventually fallen asleep because I woke up the next morning to thunder rolling across the world hard enough for my bed to shake. At first, I was sure that the phone call had been nothing more than a vivid dream, a nightmare I'd managed to conjure up, but it wasn't long before reality set in and I realized it had been real after all. The *real* nightmare was the one I lived *before* I went to sleep.

That day ended up being the first day of a new level of misery for me. The world seemed to close even tighter around me each time I had to leave the house, something I tried to avoid at all costs whenever possible. School became a blur, sometimes, the classes more torturous than the time out in the playground. It was during one of these classes that I finally snapped.

Crying isn't a bad thing, I know that, but for a kid of fourteen living in a world where boys were expected to behave like men, crying was seen as the ultimate sign of weakness. Those who did would endure bullying on unprecedented levels for months, sometimes years, from their peers, and it followed them wherever they went. And yet, crying seemed like the only release valve capable of easing the pressure.

The day that I finally broke, I had been sitting in Mrs. Campbell's history class, listening to her teachings on classical Roman emperors. Usually, I liked listening to her. She had this way of overdramatizing her words, almost singing the words to us as she taught her students. Her reading of The Illiad to us was one of my fondest memories of school overall, but that day, not even she could break through to me.

I'd been sitting silently for most of the class, avoiding raising my hand for any of the questions asked of the class. The truth is that I barely heard any of them; my brain was stuck in a permanent cycle of playing back every lousy episode of the past five years. Worst of all were those involving Ollie and Emma, the arguments, while rare, the ones that always hit hardest. And the more I thought about them, the more I felt the air in the room trying to suffocate me.

I felt like a kid stuck in a completely sound-proofed house, where people looking in from the outside could only see me standing silently in a room, while inside, the unbearable screams of a thousand voices tore through the air, amplified by a thousand echoes. That's how I felt sitting in class, a quiet kid three rows back staring blankly at the back of the kid in front of him while his teacher continued the lesson by reading from a textbook. The rest of the class also sat in complete silence, which was why a couple of them shrieked in horror when that usually quiet kid suddenly slammed both fists on the table in front of him and screamed at the top of his lungs before running out of the classroom.

The moment my brain snapped, it switched on some sort of autopilot, and I found myself carried out of the room and hurtling down a long corridor. The footfalls echoing off the walls were the only sound I could hear as I ran faster and faster in a desperate attempt to escape from myself. I hit the exit door with both arms held out in front of me and barely slowed as the door swung open hard, slamming into the wall behind it with a crash. I jumped down the half a dozen steps in one leap and continued running, not slowing as a bunch of seventh graders rounded a corner directly in my way. They instinctively opened up a path between each other as I ran straight for them and continued on.

I finally ended up collapsing in a heap out behind the maintenance shed near the very back of the schoolyard, my lungs burning inside my chest as I tried to suck in as much air as possible but unable to because of the sobs. The tears had begun falling long before I raced from the first building, but I had managed to flick most away before anybody could see them. Now hidden from view, I no longer cared as the emotional carnage tore through me, the sobs rocking my body with a level of violence that frightened me.

I'd cried before, of course, but always while safely hidden away from the world and usually tucked under a blanket. Not that day. That day, I sat in the open air with just a tiny building for cover as unwanted torment ripped through me. It felt like I had reached the very limit of my strength, the pressures finally robbing me of what little strength I had left. I would have gladly taken a beating that day if it meant the pain of losing my friends would vanish completely, but it wasn't to be. This was one type of pain I needed to endure.

It wasn't until Mrs. Campbell spoke that I realized she'd been standing behind me the entire time, listening to my unrelenting sobs.

"Jack, are you alright, dear?" I flinched when I heard her words, shocked that anybody was there but I shouldn't have been surprised, really. It wasn't as if I had snuck out of her class quietly or stealthed my way out of the school building. For all I knew, half the school already knew about my tantrum.

I couldn't answer her, or at least not to begin with. Just knowing she was watching was embarrassing enough, let alone me telling her why. The truth is, I didn't think she'd care anyway, waving away my reasons as easily as most of the other teachers when they heard someone's problems. But that was when she said something I have never forgotten, a revelation that still sticks with me to this very day.

"Learn to live in the moment, Jack," was what she said. "I know it's not easy, but the moment is the only thing that's real."

It took me some time to figure out what she meant, but once I did, it changed my life. The moment, the point in time that is right now, is the only real existence there is. Whatever happened in the past, no matter how long ago, be it a second, a minute, or a year, is nothing but a memory. The future, be it a minute, an hour, or a day in the future, is nothing but imagination. Most of what we consider time is nothing but a thought within our minds. The only thing that's real is the here and now, the moment we are living in right now.

As it turned out, Mrs. Campbell surprised me a second time that day when she took me aside later in the day in between classes and told me something that made me see her in a brand new light. She, too, had gone through the system back in her younger years, having been orphaned at the age of three and left without any family whatsoever. Both of her parents had been only children to their respective parents, and when they died just days apart from separate illnesses, Julia Campbell became a ward of the state.

She went one step further and told me that two other teachers on the faculty were also former members of our discreet club, and the names truly surprised me. Her telling me not only changed the relationship between us but also showed me that there were a lot more of us than I realized. It also occurred to me that those three specific teachers were the only ones who didn't treat me the way the others did, often showing a lot more empathy towards me.

I think that day proved to be a turning point for me. When I got home from school that afternoon, I ended up phoning Emma, and although it took a bit of apologizing, she finally gave in and forgave me for what I had said to her. She was right. We were supposed to be friends, and friends shouldn't judge each other. Right or wrong, it wasn't up to me to dictate her life, and if I were a friend, then I would accept her the way she was. I don't know if that's how it was supposed to work or if I was wrong for not doing more to try and save her. All I knew was that I needed her back in my life.

17

Life with Rose and her daughters became something of a record for me, eventually turning into the longest stay of my life. We celebrated the one-year anniversary of my arrival with a pizza night down at Denny's, a local restaurant Rose loved. It wasn't long after we'd gone to the same place to celebrate my fifteenth birthday, made even more special with Emma joining us. For the anniversary dinner, both of Rose's daughters, Natasha and Beth, joined us, but as usual, Ricky was away on deployment.

The thing I found strange in the house was that even after all my time living with the family, I still hadn't met Rose's son. He was always doing something with the army, either on an overseas job or just too busy chasing girls, according to his mother. There was the occasional phone call from him, but these would always be taken in Rose's bedroom, and she closed the door for privacy every time. Hindsight is a funny thing, and now, looking back, I should have known something was up, especially the way I could always feel the mood change whenever Rick's name came up, not only from Rose but also her daughters.

Life for me could have continued on in Rose's home forever if I had my way. Things were good. Great, in fact. After my explosive breakdown at school and subsequent awakening, thanks to Mrs. Campbell, things turned around for me at school, and I was finally starting to get my grades in order. My averages began to go up, not quickly, but steadily. History was still my best class, however, and the only B on my report card.

At home, I actually expanded my circle by joining a local football club. It wasn't that I loved the sport, but Emma had begun playing netball and told me it was a great way to make new friends. She also said it helped with her anxiety, and given we had that in common, I figured it was worth a shot. Who knew? I might end up showing some real talent and getting noticed by selectors.

If it wasn't for one minor change, who knew how things would have ended up for us. Perhaps I could have stayed with Rose until I was old enough to finally get my own home, starting a life I had been dreaming about for all of time. Unfortunately, sometimes it's the other people in our life who end up shaping the one we live, and when I finally met Rose's son Ricky, I finally understood why she hadn't been forthcoming with information about him.

I guess from a parent's point of view, especially one as proud as Rose, having a son in prison wasn't exactly something to share with the world, especially when said son was also a full-blown drug addict. He'd served two years for an armed burglary he carried out, his third time inside. It was an elderly couple he'd assaulted during a violent home invasion that left the husband in a coma for a week and the wife with a broken arm and a destroyed home. The crime had netted Ricky exactly forty-two quid, plus a Nokia phone that he tried to pawn and ultimately got him arrested.

The day I first met Ricky started just like any other, with me completely unaware of the change looming before me. I'd gone to school that Friday morning just as I had done countless times before. Before I left, Rose had kissed the top of my head and wished me good luck for a biology test I'd been studying for the night before. Biology wasn't really my thing, and I wasn't expecting to rank high, just enough for a pass.

When I walked into the house that afternoon with my test

proudly in hand, the tension in the air hit me the second I walked through the front door. It was strange because at first, I didn't even see anybody. There was just this weird kind of energy in the room that felt like an echo of some sort of turmoil. When I walked into the living room, already cautious, I froze when a complete stranger suddenly walked from the kitchen carrying a can of Coke and a bag of crisps.

"Ah, if it isn't the kid that stole my room," the stranger said, and I had to take a second look to see the face of Rick hidden behind a thin beard and long greasy hair hanging over much of it.

He didn't bother introducing himself, walking straight to the couch and dropping down on it without a care in the world. I just stood there, too dumbstruck to move, as I watched him pick up the remote control and flick on the television before leaning back with his snack. When he saw me still standing there, he turned his face directly at me and just stared.

"Did you want something?" he finally asked before turning his attention back to the TV.

That was when I saw Rose appear in the kitchen doorway behind him, and she waved for me to come to her. Feeling the beating in my chest still climbing, the tension in the air finally became clear to me.

"I'm sorry I haven't been honest with you, Jack," Rose whispered to me once she had pulled me to the other side of the kitchen. I could see the shame on her face, the woman unable to look me in the face. "He wasn't supposed to be out for another six months at least."

"Out?"

That was when she told me about her son, her real son, and all of the things he had done to make his family proud, starting with stealing valuable family heirlooms from his mother and selling them for a fraction of their value for his next high. He'd stolen most of his deceased father's jewellery, had beaten his mother and sisters, broken into the neighbour's home, and the list went on.

"I promise he won't be here long," she told me once she finished sharing the details, and it was a promise I would have given anything for her to keep. Unfortunately, fate wasn't listening that day.

The first change that happened, aside from Rick turning up, was me needing to move out of his room. Despite Rose asking him to move into one of the girls' rooms down the hall, he insisted on having his old room back, calling me the imposter. Rose apologized again, promised to make it up to me and ultimately had me move my things down to Natasha's room, which had sat empty for more than two years.

The next change that happened was meal times. Rose no longer cooked for the family, instead ordering fast food whenever she could. Rick lived on it, refusing to eat anything else and ensuring the rest of us followed suit. I watched Rose lose weight over the course of the next month as she barely ate and remained locked in her room most days to avoid running into her son.

Another thing that immediately changed was the number of items that suddenly began to disappear mysteriously. Each time Rose asked about something, Rick would instantly name me as the one most likely to have moved said item. When Rose asked whether Rick had taken a fifty-pound note out of her purse, he also blamed me. Thankfully, Rose knew it wasn't me. A blind man could have seen who the real thief was, and the funny thing is, most of the time, Rick didn't even bother hiding it.

Money disappearing was one thing, but when I came home one day to find that the living room television was gone, I knew things were only going to continue escalating. He was beginning to grow more confident, taking whatever he could without a care in the world. Disrespecting his mother was one thing, but to blatantly destroy her life was quite another, and I couldn't just stand by and let it happen.

The moment of truth came when I walked past Rose's open bedroom door one Saturday afternoon and saw Rick going through her wardrobe. I could only see the back of him and I stopped to see what he was up to.

"I know it's here somewhere, mother dearest," I heard him say, and that was when I realized Rose was also in the room.

I didn't walk in at first, not until I heard him speak to her. That was when I peered in to find Rose sitting in the corner of the room, sobbing silently while trying to stop the blood running from her nose. She looked up at me, and in that moment, all I could see was a soul-crushing shame staring back at me. That was when Rick flung a couple of dresses out onto the bed and saw me standing there.

"Shut the door and piss off, kid," he snapped as he pointed the door at me.

I saw red, the boiler inside me exploding in a moment of raw anger. When Rick saw that I wasn't going to follow his instructions, he began to circle around the bed, but I never gave him the chance to close the distance. I launched myself at him, screaming to let some of the pipe-bursting rage out as my arms began swinging the second we met. I got him a couple of times during that initial melee, one fist to the jaw, another to the throat, but unfortunately for me, I hadn't fully considered my opponent.

Rick might have been a junkie, but he wasn't the skinny worn down type you see hanging around the local shops begging for loose change. He'd done time inside a serious prison, and in those places, it was survival of the fittest. Not only could he ride a punch, but he could return it twice as hard, and that's exactly what he did. Rose screamed as we went at it, two lads worlds apart in body size, exchanging punches and kicks and whatever else we could launch. He picked me up at one point and threw me against the dresser. The mirror smashed into a thousand pieces, the shards raining down onto the tiled floor with an acoustic melody. I'm surprised my back wasn't carved up like a Christmas ham.

I don't know how long we went at it, but what I do remember is strong hands suddenly grabbing me from behind and pulling me back before a second set grabbed Rick. It took two police officers on each of us to finally end the fight, although we continued trying to exchange punches for a few moments longer. Rick was eventually cuffed and led downstairs while I remained in the room and sat on the bed.

Rose could have ended her torment right there and then. The police told her that if she pressed charges against her son, he would automatically be taken straight back to prison. She had the power to give us back our home and return things to the way they had been for months. All she had to do was say the words. I still remember how I felt, sitting on that bed after the officer asked her the question and listening to the silence screaming back at me. I still remember her looking down at me from where she stood leaning against the wall, a look in her eyes I had grown far too familiar with.

The sinking feeling hit me long before she ever shook her head. It continued when she looked away with that look of disgust in her eyes. She couldn't do it. She couldn't choose a stranger over her own son, no matter how bad a person he might have been. I was just the outsider, the adopted kid who could be replaced when things got better for her. I was just a temporary problem, while Rick was the lifelong commitment. The Bobbie was right. She *did* have a choice to make, only it wasn't the one he was asking her.

What happened next came as no great surprise, least of all to me. After listening to the police tell her that it would be best for one of us to leave, Rose gave the go-ahead for them to take me out of the house. She did try to apologize as best she could, and I could see that she meant it, but it didn't change the fact that I had been betrayed yet again. I don't know whether fate had played a role that night, but what I do know is that for me, it was another scar carved across my soul, the latest in a long line of permanent reminders of who I really was.

18

The two police officers who ended up driving me away from Rose's and to the first place I would ever truly feel alone couldn't have known the fragility of their escort, his vulnerabilities, or his extreme loneliness at that moment. That car ride felt more like an execution than a relocation, with my soul sitting right there on the seat beside me, waiting to finally be cut free from this mortal existence.

That first night at The Bucket proved to be yet another turning point in a long line of events that ultimately shaped the man I was to become. Listening to the events unfold just a couple of doors down during those first few hours of my three-month stay also acted as a preview of things to come. The occasional knocks on the door from prostitutes hoping for an easy score and the banging on the walls from both my neighbours; there was just nowhere for me to hide. That was one of the few times in my life when I realized that running was no longer an option. If I did, where would I go?

If you think I struggled that first night, then boy, do you have some catching up to do. That first night proved to be a snooze-fest compared to what was to come. The biggest problem of all for me was the fact I still had to survive, and to do that, I needed basic supplies. Water I had, thanks to a rusted tap in a dirty bathroom, but nutrition was another thing entirely. Food hadn't been on anybidy's agenda when they sent me to the place, and if I were going to eat, then I would have to try and find something by myself.

To a frightened fifteen-year-old kid, food didn't really become a priority until it really mattered. I spent the first two days locked inside my room, refusing to even consider opening the door to anybody, unless I knew them, of course. I would have gladly answered a knock if I knew Alison Farrow was on the other side of it. Hell, I would have even gladly swung it open for old Father Callahan at the point, but I knew neither of them would come and see me. This time, I was well and truly on my own.

It wasn't until the third day that I finally reached a point where I knew I had no choice. My hands had begun shaking from low blood sugar, and my insides felt like they wanted to cave in on themselves. I needed to find food, and with no money to buy some, I knew my options were limited. This was the moment I had been dreading since arriving at the place. It was time to meet the locals.

When I finally made the decision to venture out, I spent another five to ten minutes standing at the door, staring down at the key in the lock and wondering whether I could somehow avoid leaving the room. The thought almost made me smile at its sheer stupidity. It wasn't as if I could phone for a pizza and patiently wait for it to be delivered to me, although the idea did sound appealing.

It took all of my courage to finally reach forward with my shaking fingers and twist the key until I heard the lock slowly slide back. As if needing confirmation, I relocked the door and then repeated the process, further delaying the inevitable. The handle itself felt cold to the touch, and I left my fingers resting on it to see how long it would take for them to warm the metal up. When I finally closed my eyes and took a deep breath, I broke through the fear and opened the door.

What hit me almost immediately when I slowly pulled the door back was the wall of stench that immediately streamed in, a damp moldy stink supported by the hint of dope. At first, I second-guessed my decision, but then my stomach grumbled as if to remind me of the reason we were taking the chance to exit the room.

I still hadn't pulled the door wide enough for me to walk through, but when two guys suddenly walked past, their appearance scared the absolute crap out of me and I instinctively pulled the door open the rest of the way. You might have assumed that I'd try to close it, but I didn't want to portray weakness. I wanted them to think the exact opposite, and so I pretended to be casually opening my door.

They didn't even look at me or acknowledge my presence at all. It was as if I didn't exist, and my opening the door had occurred in another realm entirely. They simply walked past side by side and disappeared down the hall. Once their footfalls faded out, and I was sure they weren't waiting for me around the corner, I slowly stuck my head out and grabbed my first proper look of the hallway where I heard so much commotion throughout the previous couple of nights.

To my surprise, the place looked deserted; not a single person was visible where I had heard several voices before. Doors ran down both sides of the corridor, and while the walls had some minor graffiti in places, it wasn't quite as bad as I had feared. The floor did have this weird beige-looking carpet that might have been new sometime during the Thatcher years, but other than that, it looked fine.

Suddenly remembering where I was, I turned back and took the key from my door, closed it, and made sure to lock things up. I didn't have much, but what little I did have needed protecting. If I lost the room, there would be nowhere left for me to go but the streets and I wasn't about to take that risk.

With the key safely tucked into the pocket of my jeans, I headed to the end of the corridor, retracing the steps I'd taken three days earlier when in the company of the police escort. This time, there was nobody to help me. As if to will me forward, I heard a door open somewhere behind me but didn't dare take a look. Footfalls began to get closer, someone a lot heavier than me making several of the floorboards beneath carpet groan in protest. Picking up speed, I tried to get to the door well ahead of the mystery person, and when I finally pushed myself out into the day, I immediately wished I had reconsidered my decision.

The scene outside the building looked like something out of a movie, and not the kind spreading cheer. Multiple groups of people congregated around drums holding fires, several warming their hands while engaged in conversation. I watched white tendrils of vapour rise from their lips each time they spoke, much of it eventually intermingling with cigarette smoke before rising above the crowd in an ever-fading cloud. At the mouth of an alley, several guys stood around talking loudly, one in particular laughing loudly each time one of the others spoke. A mangy-looking dog lay near the feet of one of the men, its ribs sticking out an indication of its condition.

Nobody turned to look at me. For a second, I stood in the same spot near the entrance, wondering if I was really there, but then I heard my previous pursuer push through the door behind me.

"Watch out, kid," the old guy muttered as he tried to step around the limited space on the steps, and I had to move to one side to keep from getting knocked over. His annoyance at me proved my existence in the space.

Turning back to the greater area, I tried to detect any possible sense of direction for me to take, which firstly removed me from what was an extremely uncomfortable situation and, secondly, would help me find food. Scanning the outer edges of the place, it appeared to have just two ways in, the alley guarded by the group of men and their dog, and the other side of the courtyard where I could see several junkies shooting up.

While they appeared far scarier than the junkies, I opted for the group of men and their dog, mainly because I figured the dog would have a better sense of where the real threat was. If it was comfortable with the group, then so was I. As it turned out, I needn't have worried. They barely noticed me at all as I walked past the group. Just one of them looked in my direction and even gave me a bit of a head nod as an acknowledgement. I returned it just to be sure he didn't get offended.

The alley ran directly past the south wall of the Bucket and out onto Atlantic Road, which ran parallel to the train lines. Once out on the street, I turned to where I thought the most road noise came from, and a few blocks down, I came to the first lot of shops. Given the clear sky above, there were quite a lot of shoppers out and about, and I figured it would make my job just a little easier.

I guess now would be a good time to tell you about survival, or at least the kind I needed to practice. Given my situation and those I'd been caught in previously, it's not always possible to follow the letter of the law. Sometimes, it's the will to survive that drives us to do things we may not always be proud of, and for me, stealing was one of them. I'll be honest and admit that this wasn't the first time I needed to steal food to survive, and it might surprise you to learn that even committing criminal acts comes with its own rules. Yes, thieves with morals have rules.

For one, I would never steal from a child. No matter how desperate I became, I refused to lower myself to such a disgusting level. To me, kids were off limits. I also refused to steal from businesses run by families, the small corner shops where a mother and father might be working together. It just felt wrong to be stealing from battlers, which is how I saw them.

If I needed to eat, the best places I found were the dumpsters out behind some of the bigger supermarkets. Sometimes, you'd find the freshest food in them or recently expired packets that were still perfect in every way. If I got really lucky, I might even find myself some treats, like day-old fresh donuts or cakes. When the pickings were slim, it was just a matter of time until the next round of wasted produce showed up. All a person needed was a bit of patience and the courage to go and get it.

It was better to go food hunting at night, especially right on the cusp of dusk, just after the sun had gone down. That was when a lot of the supermarkets, those who closed their doors around eight o'clock, would begin to unload the wasted stock. You could keep an eye on them from a distance, and once they finished dumping everything and closed their back doors again, you knew it was time to go.

It wasn't unusual to run into competition. Some nights, if you were lucky, you might come across people willing to help, and together, you'd team up to find food. Those times were rare, though, and usually required one to risk exposing themselves, something I rarely did. I had been caught out on one occasion back when I ran away from Whispering Hall one time, where my supposed helper ended up taking everything we'd accumulated, slammed the lid of the dumpster down on top of me and left me there alone.

When I went out looking for food the day I emerged from Brixton House, I didn't have the benefit of nightfall on my side, nor the street smarts about the area. Brixton, to me, could have been in the middle of Australia, a virtual mystery. I hadn't had enough time to scope the place out completely, and that meant I was walking blind.

I walked several blocks in several directions until I came across a Tesco, which I thought might have looked ripe for the picking. Its dumpsters stood at the very bottom of a laneway that appeared to be shielded from the main road and nosey onlookers. I figured if I timed it just right, I might manage to score something worthy of lunch. The only issue I had was a small group of guys standing just near the mouth of the alley. Unlike the group with the dog, these guys looked to be a lot younger, and I knew that meant trouble.

Young guys, especially ones who appeared to spend more time on the streets than whatever place they called home, usually thrived on what I called pack mentality. With plenty of testosterone flowing between them, they usually felt a need to one-up each other, proving their manhood to try and take the place of the Alpha male. This could take the form of anything from harassing some pretty girl walking past, stealing something significant, or beating up some unfortunate loner who just happened to be nearby.

In this instance, I would become that unfortunate loner if they spotted my trying to get to the dumpsters, and even if they didn't pounce on me then, I had no doubt they'd jump at the chance to pick on some poor kid looking for food in a bin. There was no way they would let that slide, which meant my chance of getting anywhere near the back of that alley in the immediate future was slim to none.

I watched them for a few minutes as one of their number went to town, kicking a fire hydrant multiple times in an attempt to unscrew one of the large caps. The others just watched, occasionally giving him a cheer whenever he missed. I considered going to try and find another supermarket, but my stomach growled again, the feeling of hunger turning to sick. The thought of just walking into the supermarket itself and stealing something off the shelf crossed my mind, but I didn't want to risk getting caught. My freedom was worth far more than a random meal.

Yes, but if the bobbies pick you up and take you to jail, you also get food, a voice in my head cried out, but I quickly pushed it aside. No amount of food was worth losing such an essential part of me.

I was about to resolve myself to trying to find some other supermarket nearby. Areas that had one usually had a second close by, and if I didn't find one, then I would double back and see if the group had moved on. Either way, I knew I had to go. But just as I turned to leave, I heard a voice in the distance suddenly call out in a way that immediately drew my attention.

"Tally ho, lads," that voice shouted as one of the group began to run the opposite way for a few steps before turning back. The accent was undeniable, the Scotman imitating an Indian one of a kind. It was Ollie.

With a renewed sense of urgency, I ignored the threat of getting jumped and walked towards them, only second-guessing myself halfway across the street when several of them turned to look at me. I still couldn't see my friend amongst them but was positive it had been him shouting in that voice.

"Check out this geezer," one of the others said, and two of the guys who had been tinkering with the fire hydrant looked up at me. I felt my cheeks begin to burn but pushed on regardless. That was when a new face appeared between two of the bigger lads near the back of the group, one I immediately recognised. His hair might have been a lot longer and the acne more pronounced but it was Ollie.

"Well, I'll be buggered," he said as he stood upright. "Look at what the day brought with it."

He didn't exactly run at me on account of needing to keep his reputation intact, but he did give me an almighty slap on the back during our brief hug.

"Guys, this is Jack," he told the rest of his friends, who each shook hands with me in turn. One of them preferred the fistbump, while another just kind of waved at me with a sheepish grin. Once I had been introduced, Ollie made his exit. "Catch you guys later."

"Fancy running into you down here," I said, once we were a bit down the road.

"I know, right?" He gestured for us to cross the street. "How did you end up in this dumpster party?"

I told him about my previous home and how the son had walked in and screwed everything up. Ollie listened as he fumbled a smoke from his packet, flicked it into his mouth and lit it. I stopped once I shared the part about getting sent to Brixton House, and he began waving a hand at me.

"Are you serious? You're staying there?"

"Yeah, why? Is that bad?"

"That's where *I'm* staying," he cried out and then, as if to remind me of who he was, added, "Tally-ho, chap, we share the same lodgings," in his best Scotsman's voice.

When we reached the other side of the road, he stopped to tie his laces, and while crouched down, he heard my stomach growl, the sound continuing for close to half a minute.

"Christ, kid, when was the last time you ate?" he asked as he pushed himself off the ground.

"It's been a while," I admitted.

"OK, then, let's get you something to eat."

Turning back towards the front of the supermarket, I first thought that Ollie was going to lead me inside and steal something for me. As much as I didn't want him to, the hunger pains weren't letting go, and so I blindly followed him towards the front door, but when he reached them, he actually continued on and ended up walking into an adjacent bakery.

That was one of the few times when Ollie actually surprised me in a good way. He pulled a small bundle of notes from his pocket, separated a tenner from the pack and proceeded to buy a variety of rolls and pastries that came in three separate paper bags. Once he handed me the bags to carry and grabbed the other one filled with a couple of Cokes, we headed back out towards the street before he turned to me.

"What do you say we take these back to your place?"

"Sounds like a plan," I said, and off we went, heading back to the very place where I still didn't know if I really wanted to be.

Along the way, Ollie updated me on his life and the incident with the stolen car. He said that he got held in juvenile detention for a couple of weeks before the magistrate gave him a suspended sentence. I couldn't believe how lucky he'd been. Our conversation also highlighted the fact of how little we'd been keeping in touch, given that I hadn't heard about the outcome of his case or even bothered to find out. I felt bad but knew I had plenty of things going on in my own life. While Ollie was one of my closest friends, we both understood the world we lived in. Sometimes, we had to focus on ourselves just to survive.

"You know, Emma is living just a town over," he told me when we reached the alley near Brixton House.

"Really?" I was surprised. "I thought she was still in Hackney."

"Hackney?" He looked at me, confused. "Em's never lived in Hackney."

"You sure?"

"I'm sure, brother. She's over in Peckham. Been there for about a month now."

I shook my head in disgust, disappointed that I'd let my friendships slip. It felt wrong after everything we'd been through. Ollie noticed and clapped me on the chest.

"We're friends for life, Jack, remember? For life."

"I remember," I said, recalling the promise we all made on that long-ago beach, back when it still felt like we could conquer the world. That small pipedream continued to diminish each and every year, but the promise did not. Or so I hoped.

We reached the room, and after I unlocked the door and let Ollie in, he dropped the bag of drinks on the counter before rushing off to find the bathroom. I waited until his return before opening up the bags of food. Once I bit into the first roll, there was no stopping me; the true extent of my hunger was finally unleashed.

We ate in silence. Despite having more than enough for the two of us, Ollie barely ate the one bread roll he picked from the bag, the only thing he nibbled on. It wasn't until I had devoured four bread rolls, a couple of the Danish pastries, and half the Coke that I finally slowed down. I didn't stop, but I did slow the rate of consumption down to just a couple of bites a minute as I continued listening to Ollie share his story, a story I will share with you at a later stage.

It was after my belly had been filled and while listening to him that I finally got a good look at my friend, and I immediately found myself saddened by the sight. I didn't come out and say anything, although sometimes, I wish I had. Maybe my words might have changed the course of his story, although I remembered the one time I did try to intervene. Things didn't end so well for us.

He'd lost weight, and not just a little bit. Gaunt isn't exactly how I would have described him, but I did notice some of his bones definitely making an appearance. His eyes looked sunken into their sockets, faint dark circles running along the underside. His hair wasn't just greasy, but also matted in laces. I wasn't sure whether he was trying to do the whole dreadlock thing, but I didn't ask and certainly didn't have the heart to tell him that it wasn't working.

To me, Ollie looked like he was fading away, a shadow of his former self, a kid I remembered as being full of life who was now running on fumes alone. I didn't think he would die or anything like that, but I wasn't sure how much of a future he had if he continued down the path he was on. Watching him light up another cigarette, I wondered just how far into the drugs he was at that point. I wasn't sure whether he had elevated to the hard stuff already, but with the trajectory he was on, I knew it wouldn't be long before he did; that much was clear.

19

The reason why I always believed that Emma would one day turn her attention to some form of therapy is because of the way she had that instinctual ability to help people. She just seemed to know what to say and when to say it, with whomever she needed to at the time. I don't know whether it was some superpower, but I know that throughout our years of friendship, she often helped me. She was the one we turned to, be it just to listen, or for guidance, or even a shoulder to cry on when in need of one.

The first time I caught up with her again after finding myself at Brixton House came about because of Ollie, who brought her over early one Friday night the week after I moved in. She'd been out of town for several days earlier, and this was the first chance we had to meet up. Actually, Ollie never told me he was bringing her, nor the three large pizzas he carried into my room wearing the biggest grin, but before I knew it, there she was.

We hugged it out before I invited her to sit on my ratty couch that I had tried to improve by throwing a blanket over it. It didn't change the uncomfortable cushioning, of course, but it did make it a little more appealing. It was big enough for the three of us to sit on, and once we were seated, I pulled the coffee table carrying our meal closer. Never one to miss an opportunity to practice his voices, he opted for a new wizard he'd been practicing.

"Let the feast...begin," he said with an old-man gravel in his voice.

Feast we did, each of us chowing down on one slice after another as the three of us exchanged updates on our lives, relationships, and whatever else we saw fit. I didn't have the heart to tell them I was still struggling to find any source of income and had resorted to midnight runs down to some of the local supermarkets for some serious dumpster diving. I wasn't alone, either, each night catching up with familiar faces who I came to recognize in the nights to follow.

The pizzas were amazing. They weren't from one of the larger chains, but instead, Ollie had picked them up from a local place named Papa's, a kind of blended pizza/Chinese place that couldn't decide what it wanted to sell. We didn't complain and neither did the locals, once voting the place the best pizza shop in London according to some local radio station contest.

It felt good to be back amongst my friends, or should I say family. Friends isn't a strong enough word for me, to be honest. I find it lacking that deeper connection to what we had. Sitting between them and listening to their stories stirred up a lot of emotions for me, perhaps for them as well, but none of us ever mentioned them. Maybe we should have. Maybe it would have added yet another level of closeness to our already tight bond. What I do know is that there wasn't anything we wouldn't tell each other...or so I thought.

Once we finished the party, Ollie showed us his new mobile phone, a Nokia 3210, which he had bought earlier that day. Talk about me being jealous. Here I was, struggling to eat, and my best friend was walking around with a mobile phone in his pocket. As if that wasn't enough, he turned it on and showed us how to play games on it.

There were three to choose from, but the only one we ended up playing was Snake. Each of us took turns to try and beat the others' high score, and the competition between us was fierce. Emma did the best, picking up the controls a lot faster than I did and eventually beating even that master himself. We played for hours and would have probably played all night were it not for the battery finally running out of power.

With the sudden death of the night's entertainment, Ollie began to grow restless, and I could tell that he wanted to go. I think he was waiting for me to give him some sort of cue. Either that or he was hoping for Emma to make the first move, just so he didn't have to feel bad for being the first to pull the pin on the night. If it was up to me, I would have let them stay the entire night, but I knew sleep wasn't what Ollie had in mind. His constant fidgeting told me he needed a different kind of hit. When he began scratching the back of his hands, I decided to ease his suffering.

"You guys can go any time," I said. "Don't feel bad. I'll still be here tomorrow."

"Hey, you sure?" Ollie jumped at the chance. "It's just that I promised a mate to help him with something."

"No, of course not. Go, I'll catch up with you soon."

I expected Emma to follow suit and follow him out the door, but when she stood, it wasn't me she gave the goodbye hug to; only Ollie received one before she sat back down again. I walked him to the door, gave him a hug myself and then watched him walk down the hallway until he disappeared through the doors and out into the night.

"He really wanted to go," I said as I closed the door again and made sure to lock it. I'd already had a couple of incidents of people trying to get inside in the middle of the night, and I definitely didn't want it happening with Emma in the room.

"I think I know why," she said as I retook my seat, albeit on the opposite end of the couch. It would have felt weird sitting in the middle with just the two of us there.

If you think that there was any truth to that long-ago accusation Ollie made when we had our argument in the park that day, I'm sorry to dampen your expectations. While I might have had some confused thoughts about my feelings towards Emma, the thought of actually pursuing them never crossed my mind. She meant too much to me.

I had seen plenty of relationships go bust and had witnessed the utter chaos and destruction that usually followed. If I ever did give in to those teenage hormones, I would risk not only our friendship but also that of Ollie, and risking both of my friends for the sake of some romantic confusion wasn't in my playbook. I also didn't see her as someone I was *able* to pursue, even if I wanted to. Our relationship had grown beyond just friendship, and that put her on par with proper family. How could I ever have sexual feelings for someone I considered family?

"It's the anniversary today," Emma said as she double-checked her watch to be sure. I didn't have one but assumed that it was already well past midnight, which I took to mean she meant the current day.

"Anniversary of what?" I asked, wondering whether I'd missed some important event.

When Emma didn't answer me immediately, I felt a revelation coming on, some kind of news I had not been privy to at the time of creation. Instead of telling me immediately, she instead leaned forward, grabbed the bottle of Coke and poured herself a drink. As she held the cup in preparation to drink, she leaned slightly back and looked me in the eyes.

"You have to promise me you won't say anything."

"OK, a bit hard to make a promise to you about something I know nothing about, but I promise."

"Jack, please...promise me you won't make a big deal about it."

"OK, I promise," I repeated.

"Swear it."

"I swear, Jesus, Em. Want me to cut my wrist next and swear it in blood?" She ignored my sarcasm.

"Ollie made me swear never to talk about it, and I did, but you're one of us, so you deserve to know."

I honestly believed that she was about to tell me about a relationship the pair of them were having, or had, or were planning, but then that didn't make sense. Next, I wondered whether the two of them had slept together. Maybe Em had fallen pregnant, and they decided to go through with an abortion, but the way Emma kept looking at me didn't really fit that narrative.

"Ollie's aunt killed herself one year ago today."

"Aunt Vicky?"

I was stunned on so many levels. Just the fact of the news itself was enough to leave me speechless. I had met Ollie's aunt a number of times, and she'd been one of the coolest ladies I'd ever met. Funny, but a little kookie as well. Picturing her actually ending her own life was something that didn't come easy. I could have asked how she did it, but the truth is, I didn't want to know. It would have completed the vision in my head, and I don't think I would have felt any better.

Another reason I was speechless was because of the very thing I was telling you earlier, the part about Emma being the perfect shoulder for us to cry on. If you want to know why I could never imagine myself trying to have a sexual relationship with her, it's because she wasn't just my little sister, but in a way, she was also my mother...*our* mother. Emma gave us the comfort we needed, the guidance, the advice. She might have been just a kid herself, but sometimes I swear she had an old soul inside her, one that had been around the block a few times before.

The final reason I was left speechless was the confusion about why Ollie would want to keep such a huge event in his life a secret, not just a secret from the world but from me specifically. I didn't have to ask Emma to repeat herself to confirm what I already knew. The way she had repeatedly made me promise not to ask Ollie about it meant he had sworn her to secrecy just as adamantly. He didn't want me knowing at all. It wasn't as if he hadn't a chance to tell me himself. We'd spent plenty of time together, most notably just in recent days when we spent hours alone in my room. Why wouldn't he have told me then?

It turned out that I didn't have to ask; Emma was always the wiser one of us. She knew what I was thinking, probably before I was even considering it, and that's why she already knew the answers I needed.

"He didn't want you to know because he knew you had plenty of things to deal with in your own life," she said when the silence had stretched out long enough.

"But we're supposed to be there for each other," I said. "Why would he shut me out like that?"

"He doesn't see it as shutting you out, Jack, and neither do I. It's deeper than that."

"Deeper how?"

"Deeper, as in him wanting to protect you, the way you protected him that day by walking away when you did after your fight."

"The one in the park?"

"Yes, when you knew a confrontation would only hurt him more. You chose to walk away and probably saved him from dealing with more trauma." She reached out and squeezed my hand. "His problems have been going on for quite some time, and we both know they're going to continue. Ollie has accepted his fate. He knows he isn't going to ever be some high-rolling executive. He's happy if he can earn some dollars waxing cars down at the local carwash."

"That's what he's been doing?"

"Yes, why? You think he's been stealing the money?"

"To tell you the truth, I wasn't sure. I know he's still using, and I guess I just figured he was..." I shrugged, unsure of how to finish the sentence. It wasn't a thought I had put a lot of time into.

"He knows he has a habit, and for now, he's just trying to keep it under control. He doesn't even like using in front of me these days."

"His habit embarrasses him?"

"Not the way you think, no. He sees it as his own failure and feels a need to keep it separated from those he loves. He's not shutting you out, Jack. He's shutting himself out."

I was beginning to understand. OK, so I was a bit of a slow learner, but I got there eventually. I did feel somewhat guilty about doubting my friend, but thankfully, I managed to not make a complete fool of myself by flying off the deep end. Emma making me promise played a huge part in that, but as it turned out, she wasn't quite done with the surprises she had in store for me. The biggest was yet to come and would end up changing everything.

20

It was almost 2 am by the time we finished talking, and not wanting to walk home at such a ridiculous hour, Emma asked if she could stay with me for the rest of the night. I playfully scorned her for even contemplating asking such a silly question and immediately made up the bed for the two of us.

We fell asleep almost immediately, her just a few minutes before me. I did spend those moments listening to her breathing first slow, then lighten as she drifted off. We spooned for the beginning, me lying behind her with my arms wrapped around my friend for comfort. We could have stayed like that all night, but being a hot sleeper, I soon turned over and faced the door, nodded off, and had one of the best sleeps in a long time.

When I woke up the next morning, it took me a moment to first remember the night before and then realize Emma had already gone. Only the stove had a clock, and I had to get out of bed to see it. I had to check twice to make sure I wasn't seeing things because I wasn't one to sleep in. I've always been more of a morning person. It was already eleven. I barely got to the bathroom before I heard my front door open and Emma call out.

"Hey, I'm back."

"One sec," I called back, leaned over and shut the door for modesty's sake.

I don't know whether the bakery from the previous day was the locals' preferred choice or whether it was just a coincidence, but Emma had brought back a bag similar to the one Ollie and I had. Instead of bread rolls, hers held scones, complete with two little tubs of both cream and strawberry jam. She'd also grabbed us a coffee each and was already busy sipping hers when I walked out again.

"I was starving," she said as she laid out the small feast. "I didn't want to wake you."

"How did you sleep?" She looked up at me with a grin.

"Did you know you snore?"

"Snore? No way, that's for old men," I said as the tops of my ears grew warm.

"No way, bucko, you snored like a chainsaw last night. Had to kick you twice."

"I'm sorry, maybe I do."

"Yeah, well, warn a lady next time. And maybe try and keep a little food around here, Jack."

"I would if I had some money, your highness."

She surprised me by pulling out a crisp twenty pound note and holding it out to me. I stared at it for a few moments, unsure of what to do.

"Well, take it, silly." I did hold out my hand and watched Emma thrust it into the palm before turning her attention back to the scones.

"Thank you," I said as I pocketed the money, for some reason, suddenly feeling uneasy. I didn't have time to really think why before she handed me the plastic knife.

"Now eat," she said and wasted little time enjoying her breakfast.

The scones tasted amazing, the strawberry jam some of the best I'd had. The Asians really knew their stuff when it came to baked goods, and I made a mental note to remind myself to go back to the bakery if I had any leftover change. While twenty quid was extremely generous, it wasn't a whole lot in the scheme of things, not when you considered the cost of groceries and the fact I had exactly zero of anything in my room.

Emma finished first and asked to use the bathroom while I finished mine. She'd bought six scones but only ate two, and she expected me to eat the rest.

"Don't waste them, Jack," was her final instruction before disappearing behind the bathroom door, and I listened as she turned on the shower. When she emerged again just ten minutes later, I took my turn. The only toiletry I owned was a single cake of soap I'd managed to scrounge from one of the empty rooms a few doors down, and it had already been half used.

When I came out again, Emma insisted on us heading down to the supermarket so I could spend my money. Along the way, she gave me a few ideas on how to stretch it as far as possible.

"Stick to no-name brands," she told me. "And always go looking for any of those yellow Special tags you see hanging off the little flap in front of the stuff. They sometimes have really good bargains."

"No, I have to see someone nearby," she said, and sure enough, when we reached the front of the Tesco, she waved me inside after promising to meet me out the front in twenty or so before continuing on.

I did go inside but stopped to watch her walk up the street a little further before losing sight of her when she rounded a corner. I couldn't see whether it was a shop, a street, or a dark alley she'd turned down, but I didn't want to be snoopy, so I grabbed a basket and began walking around the supermarket.

I had never been much of a shopper before that day. I'd been a couple of times, of course, but Rose had never been one to check prices, and I couldn't remember Kay or Roger ever comparing brands during their weekly shops. While money was still a thing, they had enough to spread out, and shopping was one area where it didn't feel like they were stretching things thin.

It didn't take me long to understand what Emma meant about price differences between all the brands. I was surprised to find that even drinks like Coke had much cheaper alternatives. Growing up, I just assumed they were the same drink just made by someone else. They did have somewhat similar tastes but generally were the same thing to a kid. Imagine my surprise carrying extremely limited funds that I could twice as many of one variety compared to just a single of another. And soon, the basket began to fill.

While I would have loved to have gone nuts, I had to play it smart. My room wasn't exactly overflowing with flashy new appliances, so my choices were limited. I did have a microwave, as well as a kettle. I also had an oven, but it didn't work, and neither did the stove top. Sunday roasts weren't going to happen any time soon, but I did grab a few packs of 2-minute noodles, some boxes of mac and cheese, and a few other staples. I also checked out the prices of toothbrushes, found the cheapest one I could find and added some no-name toothpaste.

Emma found me just as I finished walking down the toiletries aisle and helped me with a couple more things before we headed for the register. Her mood had picked up considerably, and she told me that she might have a proper job soon working at a nearby cafe. Her news added yet more pressure on me to find my own, but I didn't let it show. I didn't want her thinking that I was jealous or anything, especially after her helping me out the way she did.

When we reached the register, I immediately felt my cheeks burn with embarrassment when the total came to £20.38, and I only had what Emma had given me. Before I had a chance to react, she casually pulled a few coins out of her pocket and handed them over, ignoring my reaction completely. I whispered a thank you to her, and once the stuff was packed, we each grabbed a bag and headed out into the day.

We ended up spending the rest of the day together, first enjoying the finest two-minute noodles I'd ever made (*insert sarcasm here*) and then sitting down on a dry bit of concrete at a nearby basketball court. We spent hours talking about how our lives might look ten years down the track, sharing visions we'd had of our own futures. Much to my surprise, Emma began to share a dream she'd had for

years, one where she got to help people within her very own coun-
selling centre.

"I want to help people, Jack. People like us, kids with nowhere
else to turn. I want to give them a place where they can come and just
let their bottled-up emotions go without judgment."

I still remember the look she had in her eyes, one of complete
determination, a hint of underlying sadness sitting right behind. I
think that sadness was for herself, and for me and Ollie, and all the
others that never had a place like that, kids forced to carry their own
scars and keep them hidden from a world disinterested in them.

"Is this a private therapy session, or is anybody invited?" a
familiar voice interrupted us a little after three, and I looked up to see
Ollie standing behind us.

"Get your butt down here, mister," Emma said and patted the
grass next to her. Knowing better than to ignore such an invitation,
Ollie pretended to stumble as he walked over, fell down, and rolled
sideways a couple of times until he lay next to us, his face supported
by one hand and him looking mighty pleased with himself.

"At your service, ma'am," he crooned in a grandfather voice.
Emma just giggled.

The three of us sat there until the final rays of sunlight disappeared behind the nearby buildings, the air turning cold almost
immediately. Ollie was first to his feet and held out a hand to each of
us. When on our feet again, we practically ran back to Brixton House,
keen to see what other concoctions Chef Jack had up his sleeves.

If anybody had really been expecting a feast, then they were in for
quite a disappointment because mac-and-cheese mixed in with
chicken-flavoured noodles isn't exactly a delicacy worth writing
home about. But I was tired of always scrounging off my friends and
didn't want them forking out for more pizzas or burgers. I think they
both understood, which was why they quietly accepted my hospi-
tality and pretended to enjoy the food.

We continued chatting as we ate, and once we finished, Ollie pulled
out a small bottle of bourbon that he'd been hiding in his jacket pocket.

"Let's get warmed up, shall we?" he said as he held it up for us to see.

I had never been much of a drinker, but not because I was a prude. For many, drinking helped them escape from the reality of their lives for a brief moment in time. I've seen people get absolutely plastered, drinking themselves into oblivion with the hope of escape and end up in a much worse situation. For me, it had never been about escape. To me, drinking took away the only control I had, the one power I needed to keep myself safe. I didn't like the thought of alcohol impairing my ability to control a situation, and I had seen what happens when someone loses themselves in the drink. Ollie's aunt was a prime example.

Not wanting to be a complete stick in the mud, I agreed to just a single shot and regretted it almost the instant I felt the uncomfortable burning in my throat. Ollie began to laugh when he saw me turn red and try to hold in a cough as he took a second swig directly from the bottle and grinned wide enough to show teeth.

"All in the wrist," he mused.

Emma had hers mixed with coke, the way I should have had mine, and drank it far more casually, still working on her first as Ollie worked his way through the bottle. I wanted to speak up, maybe to try and slow him down, but I knew it would only lead to conflict, and the last thing I wanted was for us to end up in another argument. So, I let him go, focusing on our conversation instead, or at least long enough until he began slurring his words and eventually falling asleep on the couch.

The night could have ended there, and I would have been content with how the day had played out. I'd had fun, in a grown-up kind of way, hanging out with my friends and just getting close the way we did when we were younger. Little did I know that things were about to take a decidedly dark turn and definitely not in a direction I ever saw coming.

When Emma finished the rest of her drink with one final swallow, she first held the cup to the side of her face while staring at me. I didn't notice her look at first, watching Ollie's hand as it repeatedly twitched as if caught in some dream-like theatrics. I was about to point it out to Em when I noticed her watching me.

My initial thought was that she had changed her mind about the whole no-sex-between-friends thing and she was contemplating jumping my bones. Honestly speaking, I'm not sure how hard I would have resisted, given the raging hormones racing about my fifteen-year-old body, amplified further by the recent sip of alcohol. But that thought only lasted a split second as I remembered who she was: Little Miss Reliable, someone I knew who respected boundaries, or at least *some* boundaries.

When she slowly set the glass down and then kept a hold of it for a moment longer while staring down at it, I could see whatever she was thinking weighed heavily on her. It was a decision she was contemplating, one that she wasn't sure she was ready to make.

"What is it?" I asked as she looked over at me again.

That was when she reached over to her jacket, pulled it closer and reached into the inside pocket. When she pulled a small black make-up pouch, I felt an uncomfortable tightening in my middle.

"Just don't judge me, Jack," she whispered as she opened the pouch and what she pulled out shocked me in a way I still feel to this day.

The small, clear bag of white powder was what she pulled out first, followed by a syringe, a teaspoon, and a lighter. Next, she reached over and took Ollie's cigarette packet out of his shirt pocket, snatched one out and broke off the filter.

"Em?"

She didn't look at me, continuing to prepare her hit like a seasoned pro. I watched in awe as a girl I had known for years suddenly turned into a complete stranger, transforming before my very eyes. The way she carefully sprinkled the white powder onto the spoon, flicked the lighter to life, and then watched as the heat turned the contents into what she saw as liquid joy. Next, Emma dropped a small chunk of the cigarette filter into the liquid, grabbed the syringe and pulled back the plunger. I watched as the needle sucked every bit of that meth up into the tube, leaving nothing behind.

Next, Emma held the syringe in one hand, dropped the spoon onto the table, and then stood up to remove her belt. Once off, she sat back down, and just before she went to tie the strap around her arm, she stopped and looked at me. I felt my jaw hang open, powerless to close it as our eyes met. That was when she did something I couldn't have predicted, ultimately changing the night's course. She held the belt up to me.

"Want to try?"

It felt like the silence between us had begun consuming time itself, seconds feeling like minutes as the moment stretched out. Our eyes locked, mine unable to pull away as a thousand questions continued racing through my head. While I had been so focused on Ollie and his addiction, I never even considered the possibility that Emma might have had one as well. It didn't make sense, none of it. Smoking dope was one thing, but to be shooting up like a seasoned addict, quite another.

"Em," I finally managed to whisper, but the real nightmare for me was that I suddenly realized I didn't know how to knock back the offer. Something about that moment felt out of my control, an overwhelming force pushing me toward an unfamiliar choice that I never considered I'd have to make.

"It'll make you fly," she whispered as she slid ever so slightly closer, held out her other hand and waited for me to give her mine.

My arm felt disconnected as I watched my hand suddenly rise from my lap and reach out for hers, dropping into her palm before relaxing again. The warmth of her skin sent ripples through me, but that was nothing compared to what was to come. I watched her push the sleeve of my t-shirt over my shoulder and then loop the belt around my upper arm a couple of times. When she gave it a final squeeze and tied it off, our eyes met again, this time Emma adding a mischievous grin.

"Does it hurt?"

"Just a pinch," she whispered, tapped the inside of my elbow and flicked a vein with her finger a couple of times. "And then you float like a feather."

It didn't feel real as I watched her take the syringe and slowly push the tip of the needle into my vein. The pinch only lasted a bare speck of time, noting compared to the lifetime of dread I was sure would follow. She pushed the plunger down just a fraction, barely enough for the icy death to touch my insides, before drawing blood into the tube. I watched the bright red droplets dance with each other for a few brief moments of panic before disappearing back into the needle. A cold flush suddenly gripped my arm, paused, then rushed up into my shoulder. I felt my chest tighten as chills seemed to gravitate out from my middle, the hairs on the back of my neck all standing to attention like a thousand soldiers on parade.

I closed my eyes as the room faded into the background of existence. I remember hearing Emma's voice telling me to enjoy the ride, but the final syllables vanished into a void filled with warmth. An intoxicating tingling began to form somewhere behind me, way down in the very base of my spine. Waves of pure electricity began rippling along every single nerve in my body, all coming to life like a Christmas tree. I felt...alive...alive in a way I never thought possible. My body felt switched on in every way imaginable, an awakening, if you will. The pulses of ecstasy rushing through me took me to another plane of existence, an existence I never wanted to leave.

21

"GET THE HELL OUT OF BED," a voice screamed somewhere above me, and despite trying my hardest to open my eyes, the lids refused to respond. I could hear more shouting from somewhere beside me, but something in my brain felt switched off, unable to wake the rest of me up. That was when strong hands suddenly grabbed me by the arm and dragged me off the bed as a familiar voice began screaming out in protest.

The cops didn't need to kick the door down, as it had already been unlocked. By the time I did finally manage to force my eyes open, Ollie had already been cuffed, two cops trying their hardest to drag him out into the hallway.

"What the hell is going on?" I shouted above the noise, trying to make myself heard, but their attention wasn't on me, and I watched as they finally managed to unhook Ollie's feet from the doorway and pull him out of the room. Once he was gone, those left in the room turned to me.

"Your friend is going to jail, you hear? Now, who are you?"

I gave them my name and details, and while one of them ran my information through whatever system they were using, a couple of the other officers began searching through all the cupboards and drawers, as they searched every inch of my room.

"I don't have anything," I tried to tell them, but none of them paid me the slightest attention.

That was when I first noticed Emma's absence. I tried to look past an officer near the bathroom door but knew that from the way they had already cleared the room, the chances of her being in there were zero. She had also taken her jacket and been smart enough to remove any evidence of what we had been up to, another sign that she wasn't an amateur, unlike Ollie, who left the empty bourbon bottle lying open and on its side atop the coffee table.

"Your friend won't be back anytime soon," one officer said as he walked back into the room before turning his attention to one of the others and whispering something into his ear. He, in turn, gestured for the others to leave by cocking a thumb to the door. "Enjoy your day," the first one finally said before walking out of the room and leaving me alone to contemplate my next move.

The veil of brain fog that I struggled against when first woken up by the police officers remained hanging in my head like a congealed mass of confusion. I had to look down at the needle mark on my inner elbow to make sure it hadn't just been some horrible nightmare. The reddish pinprick stared back at me with an evil grin, letting me know that I had lost my pact to remain clean for life.

Just to be sure it was real and not some super-persistent strawberry seed, I reached down and touched it, carefully scraping my fingernail across it and hoping to pry it free. It didn't move, the faint bite of uncomfortable pain reaffirming its existence. If the mark was real, then so was the rest of what I hoped to be a dream. It was a confirmation that hit me harder than you might imagine, a momentary lapse of judgement costing me one of the biggest promises I ever made to myself.

To help you understand why, I have to go back a bit, just a couple of years to when I went through a particularly bad spell. It was during my second time at Whispering Hall and right before my second escape from the place. I remember it so easily because it was the first time I ever truly learned about my past, the one before I became a ward of the state.

Alison Farrow wasn't an easy person to get a hold of when you didn't have access to a phone or postage stamps. She only visited the building on odd occasions and never announced her intended arrival ahead of time. I'm sure Father Callahan and the rest of the priests knew, but not us kids. I managed to draw her attention one rainy autumn afternoon just as she walked out of Father Callahan's office, and when she walked over to me, I asked her if there was any way I could find out some information about my mother.

At first, her disingenuous smile faded as she listened to my request, and after considering my question, she said that it might not be possible.

"A lot of the time, those records are sealed for your protection," was what she told me, but I couldn't take no for an answer, not after everything I had already been through. "You can request them when you turn eighteen, however," she quickly added, but again, it wasn't what I wanted to hear.

"Please, I need to know," I pleaded. "Just her name."

I hated knowing that all the information was right there in my head, locked away behind a wall of childhood trauma and time. I heard one of the older boys tell one of the others that he wanted to undergo hypnosis to unlock past memories about his parents, but I wasn't sure whether something like that would have worked for me. Alison Farrow seemed like the next best thing.

"I'll see what I can do," was what she finally said to me, and without waiting for a reply, I watched her turn and walk out of the building.

For three weeks, I waited for something to come of it, and for three weeks, I was sure that she'd either forgotten or just didn't want to help. That was until the first Monday of the new month, when she delivered a new arrival for the Hall and a small slip of paper for me.

"Just know that this isn't a regular thing, Jack. We're trying to save you from opening up old wounds, OK? Past trauma can be very destructive for some people, and your transition wasn't an easy one if I remember correctly."

"I just need to know who my mother was," I said, and she smiled at me in a way I can still feel, an empathic look in her eye that showed a faint glimpse of her soul.

While the slip of paper gave me her name, it wasn't enough for me to find out the rest of the backstory. For that, I had to wait another two weeks until our class made its fortnightly walk down to the local library where we each got to spend an hour or so searching for a book to take back with us to read over the following couple of weeks. I found my book quickly, a lot faster than usual, because I had other things on my agenda.

The library kept a complete catalogue of old newspapers in its archives, and after lying to one of the assistant librarians who always walked along the aisles returning books to their shelves, I managed to get what I needed. I used the old fake-project lie, the one about me working on an important school project about a particular moment in time.

I'll save you the unnecessary details about the subsequent search, but after just forty minutes of searching, I found what I was looking for. Using the death notice as a starting point, I managed to track down the details of a woman I could barely remember, a face that had only appeared to me in dreams. Jennifer Eileen Hardy died of a heroin overdose three days before her twenty-second birthday, a birthday she shared with me. The words hit me like bullets, each harder than the one before. As tears began to fill my eyes, I understood what Alison Farrow meant about protecting us from further grief.

Sometimes, I wish I hadn't asked her for my mother's name, that the illusion of who she was remained intact so that I could start fresh, if you will. A blank slate for me to work with. Finding out that she had an addiction hit me hard, especially to a kid as clueless about the whole thing as I was. I remember promising myself that I would never allow myself to fall into the trap of drugs the way she had, that I would be the one to stop the cycle.

The next time I ran away, I managed to find my way to the cemetery where she lay. Standing before a grave holding someone as significant as your mother is an experience in itself, one that I found myself completely unprepared for. It felt so surreal to finally be so close to her, and yet so far, unable to reach out and touch her mortal remains. There was no photo on the headstone like a couple of others because there was no headstone, just a tiny metal plate fixed into the concrete base.

I sat in front of her grave for hours in silence, just picturing the life we could have had if it weren't for some foolish choices. That was the thing most people forget. They see a drug addict, think of them as nothing but a worthless junkie without seeing the path that led them to it. I sat with my mother, wondering what kind of struggles she went through to end up where she was, the pain and torment she faced. Was I one of the reasons she ended up how she did?

The time I spent at that grave is what I saw as my first ever soul search. I tried to see how I could make sure that I didn't follow her down the same path the way many kids often did with their parents. I made a promise that day, not to my mother, but also to me, a promise that I kept until the night Emma gave me an offer I was too weak to decline.

As I sat on my couch that morning, I came to accept that I had broken that promise. I could see how people got hooked on the stuff, recalling the way it had made me feel the previous night. That unbelievable buzzing in the base of my spine still tingled at the sheer thought of it, and a sudden urge to repeat the game washed over me. I think if Emma had been with me at that very moment and she had the gear to make it happen, the urge would have been too great to ignore.

"Never again," was the promise I made to myself instead, whispering the words into the air as I looked up to the ceiling. "I promise, Mum. Never again."

I don't know whether she heard me or not, but I knew that it didn't matter if she did. *I* heard it, and that was the important thing.

In a way, breaking my pact the first time highlighted to me the lesson behind it. If I learned from it, then it hadn't been a failure after all.

22

It took me a bit to get through the self-reflection, but once I was sure I was back on track, I began to wonder where Emma might have gone. With nothing else to do, I figured that I might as well go and see if I could find her so I could share Ollie's arrest with her. It wasn't as if I could go and help him. I had her home address, and since it was only like a half-hour walk from The Bucket, I figured it would do me good to get a bit of fresh air and try to clear out some of the cobwebs.

Once out in the day, I wondered whether the sun was such a good idea when the blinding rays nearly burnt through the back of my retinas, their intensity amplified by some of the left-over snow. I think that might have been one of the first times in my life when I craved a pair of sunglasses. I'd heard about hangovers plenty of times and wondered whether meth left users with a similar reward.

Two streets down, I watched a police car fly down the road with lights and siren blaring, a few others stopping completely to watch. After spending the last few days in the place, it wasn't a foreign sound to me, with sirens being quite a common occurrence. The car didn't seem to slow as it sped past, eventually disappearing from view around the next bend.

While I knew Emma's address, I hadn't actually been there before, and with my limited knowledge of the area, I ended up having to ask for directions. The first shop I popped my head into, the hairdresser busy working on an old lady, told me to buzz off and annoy someone else. The snicker from the client was what embarrassed me the most, but I didn't let it bother me too much. The second shop, a laundromat run by an Asian couple, proved far more helpful, the man even coming out onto the footpath to point me in the right direction. I had been on the wrong street but headed in the right direction.

I had to double back to a laneway, follow it for three streets, turn left, and then the next right was Edison Way. When I eventually reached it, I found Emma's house as the third one along, and not at all what I had been expecting. The front yard reminded me a bit like the one I'd seen at Aunt Vicky's the day Emma and I had gone to check on Ollie. I actually wondered whether I had the right.

From what I understood, Emma had been living with some woman related to her mother...a cousin maybe? She did explain it to me, but the years have been long, and my memory is not so good anymore. It really doesn't make much difference to the events being told. What I do remember is that the woman worked as a bartender down at The Pint and Pickle, a pub a few suburbs over.

When I reached the front door, I found it slightly ajar, and before knocking, I froze to see if I could hear anything. Not sure why. It just seemed like the thing to do. With only silence coming to greet me, I gave the door a bit of a tap. The echo from my fingers rasping on the timber bounced back at me, but still I couldn't hear anything.

"Hello? Emma?" Nothing. Another knock, more silence. I was considering checking out the side gate to see if I could get through to the backyard when I did hear something low and faint coming from the open doorway. "Emma?" I shouted a little louder and knocked a third time. The voice I finally heard lacked all hint of strength.

"Jjjjaaaaacckkkk," that voice called and feeling my insides tighten, I pushed the door open.

"Em, shit," I cried out when I saw her crumpled up in a heap near the back of the front room. She was lying on the floor in the middle of the doorway leading into the kitchen, and from what I could tell, she'd been beaten. The dress she had on barely covered her, the bodice torn to shreds. Scratches ran down one arm, deep enough to draw blood, and I saw bruising teeth marks on one partly-exposed breast.

"Em, Jesus Christ," I said as I knelt down beside her. She looked up at me with one good eye, the other closed over completely. A thin trail of blood ran from her top lip, the bottom one trapped between her teeth. "What happened?" I didn't wait for an answer, reaching to where the phone sat on a small table. Emma immediately reached for my arm and tried to pull it back.

"Nooooo," she managed to whisper, her voice painfully weak.

"I have to call you and ambulance." She delicately shook her head. "Em, you need help. At least let me call the police." Again, she shook her head at me.

"No, please. Just don't."

When she tried to sit up, I slipped an arm under her neck, the other under her knees and lifted her up off the floor, eventually lowering her onto the bed in the first room I could find. I propped a pillow under her head and then made sure to pull a blanket far enough to make sure she kept warm. When I was sure she was as comfortable as possible, I sat down beside her. She immediately reached for my hand and pulled it towards her chest, squeezing it tighter than I thought possible for her.

I waited until her breathing slowed down again, the rhythm eventually planing out to light snores. Only once I was sure she was actually asleep did I manage to pull my hand free and check out the rest of the house. My biggest concern was that whoever had beaten her was still inside, but given the way I found the front door, I figured it highly unlikely. Next, I wanted to try and find something to help ease her pain. I found a nearly empty packet of Nurofen in one of the kitchen drawers, grabbed a glass of water as well, and took them back to the bedroom.

Those next two hours were some of the longest of my life as I sat holding her hand, unsure of whether she would live or die. I had no idea if she had sustained internal bleeding or been drugged or what had happened to her. All I knew was that if she did die, then it would be my fault for not doing anything to help her. I considered calling an ambulance regardless, and maybe I should have, but I didn't.

When Emma eventually woke up again, she did so with a shallow groan, pausing as she tried to use one hand to brace herself enough to roll over. I held out my hand, took hold of hers and helped her sit up, propping a second pillow behind her back as she leaned against the bedhead. Next, I held up the box of painkillers. When she gave me the nod, I popped two out of the blister pack, considered the last one remaining, and popped it too before handing them over to her. She took one large swallow from the glass, popped the tablets in her mouth, and drank the rest of the water before leaning back again.

"Tell me what happened," I said as I put the glass back on the nightstand.

I expected her to tell me that she had walked in on a burglar or something, or somebody had broken in and then beaten her up so they could escape, anything that made sense. What she ended up telling was another side to a person I realized I barely knew, someone I had cherished for years and suddenly met for the first time.

She didn't tell me at first. Instead, she looked down at her hands as they rested in her lap. One of the fingernails looked torn in half, and I winced when she pulled the remaining bit off.

"A client didn't want to pay, and when I tried to get the money, he began hitting me," she finally said, doing her best to add some volume to her voice. The words didn't make sense to me at first. I was trying to figure out why a cafe client would come back to her home, having remembered her telling me about the new job she was considering. And then it hit me.

She saw the moment I understood, her eyes immediately dropping back to her fingers as they began fidgeting with each other. I finally understood more than just the injuries. It all began to fall into place, like how she could afford to give me money and buy drugs for herself, all without having a steady income from a proper job. She'd been prostituting herself, a girl of fifteen selling her body to men willing to pay for her time.

I could have yelled at her, I guess, and made her feel even worse than she already did. I could have thanked her for revealing yet another secret she'd been keeping from me, like secrets hadn't already fallen out of the woodwork these past few days. The idea that my closest friends had both been holding out on me for God-knows how long cut deep, but I pushed my feelings aside, knowing full well that this wasn't about me at all. Survival, remember?

It took Emma a bit longer to open up to me fully, but when she did, the story that followed chilled me to the bone. She told me how her guardian, a woman named Maggie something, had gone to work one night some eight weeks earlier and just never came back. According to those Emma ended up speaking with down at the pub, she'd met some foreigner travelling the world and for some crazy reason, had walked out on her life to join him. While the state essentially paid for the housing commission flat, Emma quickly needed the finances to pay for everything else, and when her options ran out, she had just a single choice to make.

I listened to Emma the way a friend is supposed to, keeping my own judgment out of it. When she cried, I held her hand; when she got angry, I let her scream. During the next two days, I listened to things that I never thought possible for a girl as strong as she was. Everything I thought I knew about her fell away as the real Emma Hardy emerged. The strong, empathic girl I always saw was, in fact, a vulnerable, scared, insecure child trying to find her place in the world, just like we all were.

I often saw Emma as a kind of leader, the one person Ollie and I looked up to because of how strong she was. How wrong we had been. I regret not being there for her when she needed me and for not offering her the same kind of strength that she had always shown me. She had been doing it just as tough as the rest of us, perhaps even tougher, and still managed to help others along the way.

For the next week or so, I took care of her. During the day, I'd head out to nearby supermarkets and find enough food for the both of us. And when her bruises began to fade, so did the shame she felt. Some nights, we'd spoon the way we did that night in my room, finding comfort in each other's arms, and I'd find us still lying like that the next morning. That was until the day I woke up and found myself alone.

23

Rather than just walk out in secret without a word, Emma had the decency to at least leave me a note on the nightstand beside me. In it, she explained that she had struggled more than she let on and that she needed to find herself again after suffering so much through the previous few months. She said that she valued our friendship more than anything else in her life and would come and find me once she healed herself mentally.

Sadness is what washed over me that morning, a feeling of utter loss. I understood why she did it, of course, having found myself in a very similar position. What saddened me most was the fact that I couldn't be there for her when she needed me most. I had always believed that true healing comes from being around family, and since we were each other's family, the place for her to heal was with me.

I believe what ultimately drove Emma to run was the shame she felt from what she had to do in order to survive. Again, I think about how much of the world tends to judge people whose lives they know nothing about. When a person has no other place to turn, sometimes the most frightening choice of all is the one to live. But while Emma had a strong survival instinct, it was her empathic side that ultimately let her down, fearing how her family would suffer because of her choices.

With nothing left for me to do at the house, I ended up grabbing the few items of food still left over, threw them into the bag and left the home for the very last time. I made sure to lock the door on the way out in the hope that if Emma should return in time, then she would find the house safely waiting for her.

When I got back to Brixton House, I locked myself in my room with a heaviness I felt powerless against. It seemed as if the tiny sliver of the world I thought the three of us had created for each other had crumbled into a smouldering ruin, with nothing left but the twisted, charred remains of a few memories I'd rather forget.

The second I sat down, I realized that I couldn't just sit back and do nothing. I grabbed my jacket and cap and headed back out into the day, desperate to find the girl who had saved me more than once. With no real direction to go, I ended up heading down to the only place where I knew she had some connection to, the Pint and Pickle. I figured she might have a contact there, some friend of Maggie's who might take pity on the girl, maybe offer her a safe place to stay.

When I got to the pub, I made it inside the first door and lasted for about two seconds before I was ordered out again.

"Oi, this ain't no place for a kid," the bartender called out to me. Some of the patrons turned in their seats to check out the boy, but I left just as quickly. Not dismayed by failing with my first attempt, I walked around to the back of the place where I knew the loading dock would be. That was usually where the staff hung out, those taking breaks from their jobs.

My hunch proved correct, and I found a couple of women sitting under a tree, smoking cigarettes. They gave me a sideway glance as I approached, and I didn't think they'd help, but when I mentioned that I knew Maggie, they immediately lowered their guard.

"Whatcha want Em for?" one of them asked.

"You her boyfriend?" the other.

"I'm just a friend," I said. "I'm just trying to find her."

I don't know whether they didn't trust me or were protecting

Emma, but neither said they knew where she was. They didn't even admit to seeing her recently, but I figured as long as they knew I was looking for her, then they might pass the message along.

"If you do see her, could you let her know that Jack is looking for her?"

"Jack, yeah right," the older woman said and knowing I wouldn't get any further, I thanked them and left.

The Pint and Pickle was just the first stop in many that day. I wasn't comfortable with just letting it go, not after the way I had found her just a few days earlier. While her body had been battered and bruised, I knew that her soul suffered the same damage, and it was that damage I was worried about the most. I needed to find her so I could convince her to get the proper help she needed.

For eight straight hours, I crisscrossed Brixton in every possible direction, checking cafes, parks, supermarkets, the Brixton Market, and anywhere where she might blend in with people. I walked by public toilet blocks waiting for her to come out and then called her name in the hope that she'd answer. I went to the train station, bus stops, and road underpasses, but found nothing. When night fell, I continued for another hour or so but knew my chances of finding her were practically zero. With all hope lost, I headed back home.

I think I ended up lying awake in my bed for the entire rest of the night, unable to sleep as I thought about my friends. With Ollie locked up in some jail and Emma somewhere out in the world trying to find herself, I had nothing left to do but try and focus on the one thing I also needed to take care of...me. I had to rebuild my life now that I had effectively been thrown out of the system and onto the streets. I had already lived a brutal existence; years of torment and abuse had shaped the man I was growing into. The question was where those types of qualities could be used.

I'm not sure at what point I ended up falling asleep, but I do know it was after the new had begun to dawn outside. My eyes felt like lead weights when I finally gave in and drifted beneath the veil of consciousness. Unfortunately, the nightmare that followed robbed me of any rest I was hoping for as Father Callahan stood at the head of the class and began screaming the names of all those I had lost along the way before writing their names on the chalkboard and forcing me to repeat them.

"You are the reason they don't want you in their lives, Jackie, my boy," he cried out, tormenting me in the worst way possible. "Nobody wants a Rag Brigade loser for a friend. NOBODY."

I don't know whether the nightmare lasted the whole night or only began moments before I woke in a sweaty mess, a final scream locked in my throat. It was still daylight outside, which meant I hadn't slept the entire day. It took a real effort for me to push myself out of bed, but when I checked the time on the stove, I found that I had only slept for four hours, both hands on the clock standing to attention.

Not wanting to waste another day moping around the room, I decided that I was going to do something I should have done days earlier. First, though, I needed to take care of some bathroom needs, mainly a shower to deal with what Emma called *boy smell*. Once I was sure I was back to a somewhat presentable state, I grabbed my wallet, jacket, and cap and headed outside.

It took me a few phone calls, but I eventually found out that Ollie was being held in nearby Feltham, a young offender prison just a few streets from where Brixton House stood. Being a Tuesday, he could also have visitors, and so, I trudged through the early afternoon rain to visit my friend. It wasn't as far as I thought, and the walk only took me about half an hour.

Getting in to see him ended up proving the impossible part, and no matter how much I pleaded my case, everybody refused to listen to me.

"I'm sorry, sport, rules are rules. Gotta have someone over eighteen accompany you in," the supervisor told me after I demanded the admin staff call one. They did, and when Supervisor Mumford showed up, he told me exactly the same thing everybody else had.

"I don't know any adults," I finally told him in a hushed voice. I looked around uncomfortably as we stood in the middle of the foyer and felt every set of eyes on me, but nobody was actually watching us. Mumford looked down at me with a look I'd seen a thousand times before. When I saw his shoulders slump just a little, I actually thought I'd won him over and he was going to give in, but it was just his frustration easing up a little.

"Anybody over 18 will do, kid, OK? I don't make the rules."

He didn't wait for me to reply, simply turning his back and returning behind the counter where he sat down at a computer terminal and began typing. I stood there watching him for a few moments before finally accepting the truth.

"Fine," I muttered to myself as I headed for the door and walked out.

Once outside, I looked at the building before me and thought about just shouting Ollie's name to see if he could hear me, but I knew it was hopeless. I had effectively been cut off from the only family I had left. With both Ollie and Emma impossible to reach, I was once again officially on my own.

24

With no place else to go, I headed back to Brixton House, and once back in my room, I sat down on the couch to think. There was little else for me to do. I had no other form of entertainment, no TV, no books, no magazines. I had a near-empty room, no food in the cupboards, and the fridge sat empty with only some stale milk I should have thrown out days before. I had no money, no form of income, no job prospects, and worst of all, no friends whom I could lean on for support. You want to see what hopelessness looks like, take a look at me right there at that very moment.

I could have gone to the dole office and pleaded my case, but the official minimum age for that was sixteen. I could have phoned Alison Farrow, but that meant going back into a system I had spent most of my life trying to escape from. The only proper choice I had left was to find myself a job. As far as I knew, both Ollie and Emma had prospective opportunities, so why couldn't I? I was of legal age, which meant there was nothing else holding me back.

What I couldn't decide on was what field I wanted to get into. I didn't have silly visions of grandeur, of course. No Wall Street broker or banking executive here. An astronaut was out to, as was that piloting dream I once had. For those types of jobs, a person needed an education, and mine was about as limited as you could get. I knew where I stood, and people like me began at the bottom...the *very* bottom.

Of course, there was also the option of going back to school if I really wanted to. Colleges were taking in all manner of special cases, and I could learn a trade, like an electrician or a plumber. Maybe carpentry was a great option, the ability to use some real tools. Unfortunately for me, I felt an urgent need to steer clear of anything that required me to sit in a room, surrounded by people, and being lectured. I knew I could have done the jobs, but it was the training to get them that I had the problem with.

If I had been in the same position a decade later, I might have opted to become a content creator, maybe grabbed a mobile phone and begin conducting video tours around some of the neighborhoods I'd hung out in, but in 2000, we didn't have YouTube or TikTok or any of the other crazy social media sites kids have access today. The only real way for someone in my situation to get a job was to get off their arse and go knocking on doors and that is precisely what I planned to do the very next day.

The place where I figured I'd have the best chance was a stretch of road just north of the trainlines where several car dealerships sat. I figured that washing cars didn't need any sort of special skill except maybe being fit, and so I thought I'd try my luck as a car detailer. I couldn't drive the things, but cleaning them was another matter. All I needed was for them to give me the rags and shampoo, and I could do the rest.

I was still trying to mentally picture myself washing cars for a living when a knock on the door interrupted my thinking.

"I don't want any," I called out, knowing that it would just be one of the half-dozen or so dealers who liked to come through and offer their wares to the tenants. Dealers and prostitutes were the usual culprits for door-to-door sales, and I had neither the money nor the need for either. When the seller knocked on the door a second time, I rolled my eyes and silently groaned. "Fine," I said as I pushed myself off the couch.

"Look, I don't want any," I said as I unlocked the door and pulled it open, and there, standing before me...was Emma.

For a second, we just stood there staring at each other, me with my mouth hanging open, of course. It took her speaking to break my paralysis.

"Can I come in?"

"Yes, of course," I said and immediately pulled the door open the rest of the way. She walked past me, the scent of perfume instantly tickling my nostrils. Not only did she smell good, but she looked worth a million quid, the bruising from her beating almost completely hidden under a layer of make-up.

She didn't sit, not even after I closed the door and offered her one. Instead, she stepped towards me and threw her arms around my neck before pulling me closer. We stood like that for a moment, just the two of us cocooned in our own unique way, letting the other one know that they were OK. When I tried to pull back, Emma tightened her embrace.

"I'm sorry, Jack," she whispered while holding me tight. "You are the last person I wanted to hurt."

"You didn't hurt me," I said, not feeling guilty about telling a little white lie.

"I know I did, and I don't think I can ever truly thank you for what you've done for me. Walking out on you was not the way to go about things."

It felt nice to be holding her but also uncomfortable while trying to hold a serious conversation.

"Can we sit down?"

"Yes, of course," she said and finally let go before following me to the couch.

"Looks to me like you might have found yourself a better situation to be in," I said as I pointed to what looked like a brand new outfit."

"I got a job through a friend at a modelling agency," she said, her face lighting up for the first time with pride.

"A modelling agency? Look at you go," I said with a smile. She tried to talk the break through down.

"It's not exactly Milan, but I'll be working with some of the top fashion models with a couple of different houses. Melanie got me a job as a runner."

"A runner?"

"They are the girls who run the pieces of clothing between the different models at a fashion show. Mel says it gets crazy busy backstage, and they usually have like a dozen girls helping out." She paused, her signature move kicking in as she looked down at her hands. "Jack, it's in Paris."

"Paris, wow, that's incredible," I said and felt genuine pride for her. She didn't see it, however, still refusing to acknowledge her own breakthrough.

"I feel bad for leaving you alone like this."

"Hey, you're not leaving me alone. I've got my own prospects to consider. I'm actually going to a few businesses tomorrow to try and get a job."

"Really? That's great. Doing what?"

"Not sure yet," I said, feeling slightly underwhelmed compared to her news. "I tried to go and see Ollie today, but they wouldn't let me in. Told me I needed an adult with me, can you believe it?"

"Yes, I can," she said. "I was actually there myself today."

"You were? Serious? How is he?"

"Surprisingly well," she said as she leaned back. "He looks almost content, in a weird sort of way."

"Ollie...content?"

"I think he's found somewhere where he might have a chance to break free from his demons for a bit."

"You mean the drugs?"

"I mean everything. The drugs, the alcohol, the people tormenting him out here."

"What people"

"The ones keeping him in that spiral downward. He told me to tell you that he's sorry for the cops busting down your door like that. He was actually expecting them, which was why he partied hard that night."

It felt good to finally be sitting down like a couple of mature adults and talking about grown-up stuff. Emma looked about as grown-up as you can get, a real woman still shy of her sixteenth birthday and finally able to pursue her dream. I was about to say so when she checked her watch and sighed.

"I have to go. My bus leaves soon."

"You're going tonight?"

"Melanie has booked us on the earliest train to Paris, and we have to be in London for it. She's waiting for me out in the taxi. I promised her I wouldn't be long." She reached over and squeezed my hand. "Are you sure you're OK?"

"Yes, I'm fine. I promise." I smiled and shook my head. "Just feels like everybody is leaving me again."

That was when she reached inside her shirt and pulled out something I wasn't expecting.

"Ollie asked me to give you this," she said as she handed over his mobile phone. "He said don't wear out the buttons playing Snake." I grinned. Then she pulled out a second phone, which she shook back and forth, "Got my own, and I've already put my number into that one, so whenever you want to talk, just call me, OK?" When she saw me trying to fight back the emotions, she leaned over and put her head on my shoulder. "I promise you that from this moment on, things will get better." I put an arm around her shoulders and hoped she was right.

Emma checked her watch again as somewhere in the distance, a very faint car horn honked. We helped each other off the couch, and just before she turned for the door, Emma again hugged me. This time, there was no talking, just the bitter silence of two friends saying goodbye. When we finished, I walked her back down the hallway and out to the waiting taxi. After one final goodbye, she climbed in and gave me a wave as it pulled away from the gutter.

I watched the taxi drive off for as long as possible, imagining her looking back at me through the rear window. Just before it disappeared around that distant bend, I gave her a wave, one I didn't know she would see. Once the taxi had vanished, I stood on that footpath and looked up into the night sky, half the moon hanging almost directly above me.

In my hand, I still held the phone Emma had given me, and when I pressed the Power button, the screen and numbers briefly lit up before fading out again. I waited for it to cycle through the power-up, and once done, I pressed the little Phonebook button. Just a single contact had been entered into it, the name staring back at me in the moonlight. *Emma Hardy* was what she had put herself in as, a name that immediately drew agrin from me. That was when I knew that things would be OK. No matter where we were in life, we would always have each other, and that's just how it was.

25

For me, life did end up getting better, just as Emma had promised it would. While I didn't have much luck the following day like I hoped I would, I did end up using the mobile phone to contact a nearby car dealership over in Croydon. It was the name of it that first caught my attention, a name with a slightly familiar ring to it.

"Hardy's Auto Group," was how the receptionist answered my call that morning, and with a grin, I told her my name and the reason for my call. "You'll want to speak to Mr. Hardy about that," she said and immediately put me on hold.

After listening to the same cycle of seven ringing bells for what felt like the most torturous five minutes of my life, a friendly voice broke through, introduced himself as Louis Hardy and asked what I was calling about. Again, I led with my name, told him about my hopes of working for him as a car detailer and then crossed my fingers when I finally stopped talking. I don't know whether he was stunned by my call or just distracted by something unseen to me, but we sat there listening to each other's breathing for more than a dozen seconds before he finally eased my suffering.

"Why don't you come down and see me tomorrow at ten," he told me and the second the call ended, I began jumping around the room like a lunatic... an *Ollie* kind of lunatic.

That night, I could barely sleep, the anxiety robbing me of any chance of a restful night. I did eventually drop off, and by some lucky miracle, I woke up feeling just as refreshed as if I'd slept for twenty straight hours. It didn't come as a surprise that the next three hours dragged by unbelievably for me; it was my fault for waking up so early. Despite living in such a small room, I still managed to pace around the place nonstop for more than an hour.

When the time finally arrived for me to head off, I did so with a definite bounce in my step. I felt good, but more importantly, I felt optimistic. There weren't many times in my life where I felt confident in seizing an opportunity, and this was about the most important one ever. If I succeeded, it could lead to me not only moving out of The Bucket for good but also to me getting my own place in a more upstanding part of town away from the kinds of people you hear about on the six o'clock news.

For the first kilometre or so, I just about ran until my lungs were close to bursting, but seeing as I made sure to leave plenty of time for myself, I took it easy for the next two. No good in turning myself into a walking sweatbox right before an interview. I had already made sure to put on some clean clothes and throw on some deodorant and needed to keep my presentation up.

Louis Hardy turned out to be far less rigid than I imagined him to be. I turned up at the dealership earlier than expected and kind of hung around the front under a tree. He must have seen me standing out there because he walked out himself to greet me and then asked whether I wanted a tour of the lace before going to his office. What I didn't know was that I already had the job in my bag; no interview was needed. After the tour, Hardy took me into his office, and before inviting me to sit, he held out his hand and shook with me.

"Welcome aboard, son," he said with that big grin, and just like that, I was a working man.

What he didn't tell me at the time but revealed many years later on the night, when he handed me the keys to the place for the last time, was that he hired me because of my last name alone.

"A Hardy is a Hardy, no matter who your parents were," was what he told me.

Not only did I get the job that day, but I also found myself a new home. After asking me about my living situation, my news boss offered me a granny flat that his daughter had built in her backyard. They were looking for a new tenant, and Hardy said that as long as I promised to show up for work each day, he was happy to pay the seventy-five quid a week for the place.

That day changed my life in a way I could never have guessed, and all because of a phone my friend had given me to mind for him. It was because of Ollie's phone that I had the means to make the call in the first place, a call I would have never made if my circumstances had been any different. I ended up working for Louis Hardy for close to ten years before he eventually announced his intention to retire. And to whom do you think he gave the first offer to buy the place?

"You'll save plenty of money with not needing to change the signage," is what he said when we eventually signed the paperwork, and it was a joke I still laugh at today.

These days, I own five dealerships, all trading in quality used cars that I make sure to keep the profit margins down on so we can keep the prices affordable for those who really need them. I have plenty of good people working for me, too, although there is one role in every location I have always insisted on keeping open. No matter how many detailers we have, I always have room for one more.

I never expected to amount to much after the start I had in life. In fact, some days, I never expected to make it to adulthood at all, and the chances of me surviving long enough are sitting close to zero. I've been back to Whispering Hall in the subsequent years, and during one visit, I even managed to lie down on my old bed. Although the mattresses and linen had been changed, the bunks themselves had not, and I ended up donating a large chunk of money to have them replaced with new ones.

I also offer traineeships within my dealerships to those old enough to apply for them, with the priests more than happy to help the boys apply. I currently have four of them working for me, three of them primed for sales positions in the next few months. I can't help everybody, of course, but there's no harm in trying to save some. If I can help change just a single life, then it's worth it.

And what about my friends, those whom I consider family? Those are stories I've saved for another day, stories that I know you'll want to read about. Like I've said before, not everybody in this world is promised a Happily Ever After, and some not guaranteed a life at all. I hope that when the time comes for me to share the lives of both Emma and Ollie, you'll be around to read about them. I know it won't be easy for me, but it's a pain I'm willing to endure to ensure we can share the rest of this journey together.

Thank you for reading the first book in this series. Before continuing with Book 2, if you enjoyed this story, could you please spare a moment and leave a review? I'm still a relatively new author, and it really does make all the difference. Thank you.

BOOK 2: CHAPTER 1

I f you think that the three of us ended up living the best lives imaginable, then you are sadly mistaken. Like I said before, real life rarely offers fairy tale endings. I think that's why we make up stories in the first place, to hide the harsh reality of life from ourselves. If I had to choose the hardest of our three lives to share, it might surprise you to learn that I wouldn't choose me at all, or Ollie for that matter. I think Emma is the one who faced the worst of it, and it was because of the letters and long-distance conversations we shared during subsequent years that I found the truth behind her forced smile.

Before compiling all of the different notes and letters into the following story, I thought I knew my friend well enough to understand her background. She'd opened up to me many times before the day she asked me to share her story, and once I agreed, I found an entirely different person standing before me. A new level of gloom consumed the facade she'd put up for most of her life. I say a facade because it takes a special kind of person to be able to hide the sort of trauma she endured not just during her later years when sitting in the middle of maximum security, but also during those early years when we would spend time together playing Mario Kart in my room back at Kay and Roger's home.

I shudder to think of what nightmares she must have carried around with her, some hiding right behind that smile of hers, the one she'd put on whenever close to people she really cared about. I think it was her way of protecting us, not that she ever came right out and admitted so. That I had to guess for myself, thanks to the multitude of conversations we had in prison visit rooms.

If it surprises you to learn that Emma ended up in prison like Ollie, then I've got news for you. Her story goes into much darker territory, darker than even some of my worst experiences. It took us many attempts to try and get the whole story out as each time we tried, the emotional scars became too much for her to bear, and we had to revisit them at a later date. I spent more time sitting in prison waiting rooms trying to get inside to see her than actually being with her. If you've never been to a jail yourself and experienced trying to get inside, then picture a medical facility's waiting room bursting with patients and half the staff missing.

The first time Emma ended up in jail was in March of 2005, just a few years after she first took that awful job in Paris. I say awful because I believe it might have been the one that ultimately sent her down the path to total self-destruction. Were it not for the isolation from her friends, she might have stood a chance to save herself, but unfortunately, it wasn't to be.

That was the first time she ever called me for help, *real* help. I remember the fear in her voice when I took the call, the kind of fear that sends genuine shivers down your spine. It was also the first time I ever heard Emma use the word beg when asking for something, as if doubting whether I was taking her seriously.

"Please Jack, I beg you," she pleaded. "Please come and help me." It had been the guarded tone that really chilled me, as if she was trying to hide the call from someone.

I had been in the middle of detailing this new Jaguar that had just come in, a 1988 XJ6 model. Louis had asked me to take special care of it as he already had a potential buyer interested in it. Personally, I'm not much of a Jaguar guy, especially that one which came in this gaudy green colour. Give me a Mustang any day.

The second I heard the phone ringing in my pocket, I knew it was her. I mean, I knew even before checking the screen for the Caller ID. I don't know if there was some sort of telepathic connection between us or what, but I just knew it was Emma and that she was in trouble. The second I answered the call, I heard it in her voice.

"I'm in trouble, Jack. Real trouble." I heard genuine panic, my own insides ramping up accordingly. "I need help. Please." She paused. I heard a kind of muffling sound before she came back, this time her voice lowered considerably. "Please, Jack. I need your help."

"Em, slow down," I said, trying to calm her down but having very little effect.

"Jack, she's dead, holy shit, she's dead. I need -"

"Em, EM." I took a breath. "Please calm down and breathe." When she paused long enough for me to speak again, I calmed my voice and continued. "Tell me what happened."

This time when she spoke, her voice sounded a lot more controlled, although still prone to jittery outbursts of emotion. I got the crux of the issue almost immediately. Emma and her friend, Melanie, had gone to a party with another friend of theirs, and this friend brought some pills with her. At some point, she asked Emma to hold them, and because of her getting a little too caught up in the fun, she forgot about them sitting in her handbag. At some point through the night, the friend collapsed, and despite attempts by paramedics to resuscitate her, she died in the ambulance on the way to the hospital. Somehow, Emma ended up being interviewed by police, and when they checked her handbag, they found the stash of pills.

Along with a possession charge, she had also been charged with manslaughter, although the prosecutor was hunting around for even more. Add to that the fact that Emma had turned eighteen just a couple of months earlier, and she was now classed as an adult, and adults served jail time in adult jails. As far as I knew, the only good thing we had on our side was that the party had been held in

London, not Paris, where the girls had been working. That meant Emma was being held on our side of the Channel.

I did finish detailing the Jaguar as best I could, but I immediately asked to leave the second I finished it. After a quick taxi ride to the police station, I sat in the waiting room, hoping to have a chance to speak with her, but of course, it wasn't allowed. The policeman manning the front desk barely acknowledged my request. It was only by sheer luck that I heard him answer a woman's question about Emma Grant that I knew she was her barrister.

"I'm Jack Hardy," I said to her when she too was directed to take a seat in the waiting room. "I heard you mention my friend, Emma Grant?"

"You know Emma?" I nodded.

"I'm guessing this isn't something that's going to get resolved today?" She surprised me with her response.

"Possibly, if I can get in to see her soon."

She introduced herself as Kelly Mann, and while she wasn't able to get Emma out of jail that day, she did manage it the following day, courtesy of an early afternoon bail hearing. I sat in and listened, no easy thing when watching one of your closest friends close to breaking point. Emma looked a frightful mess, her face screwed into mass panic as the fear ravaged her. I could see from where I was sitting that she was visibly shaking the entire time, her fingers trembling as they tried to wrestle each other for control.

When the judge eventually granted bail, I had hoped to see some of the stress vanish from Emma's face, but it didn't. She looked just as unhinged an hour later when she walked out of the courthouse beside her barrister. The second she saw me, she ran over and flung her arms around my neck before breaking down and crying. I could barely support her and had to follow her down to the concrete, where we took a moment for her to regain control.

For the next month, Emma stayed with me in the granny flat, trying to prepare herself for the possibility of doing jail time. Her barrister warned her that the case against her looked solid, and unless they could prove some mitigating circumstances, she would more than likely lose. We spoke about it at length almost every night after I came home from work, sometimes staying up until the early hours of the morning, but no matter how much I tried to reassure her that it would be OK, she didn't believe me. Sometimes, Ollie would also come over and try to talk her down, but even his advice didn't help.

Eventually, her hunch proved correct, and Emma ended up with a four-year sentence for involuntary manslaughter, a non-parole period of two. She broke down as the judge read the sentence out and had to be helped by court security. I still feel the chills run through me thinking about it, remembering the scream she let out at the moment of sentencing. A raw explosion of deep-seated fear tore from her throat and echoed across the courtroom. Beside me, Ollie physically jumped.

While we all assumed that the case had been the worst part, the real nightmare was about to begin. After already suffering through nearly every form of punishment possible, Emma was about to enter a new kind of torture, the kind she would be unable to escape from. It was only because of our subsequent talks and exchanges that I eventually found out about the real happenings behind the wall.

The words you are about to read are those from Emma herself, rewritten by me in a way that makes them a little easier to comprehend. She tried so very hard to give us a real look into the life of a girl who entered the system as a damaged four-year-old and ultimately fell to the pressures her world forced upon her. It is a story steeped in the kind of trauma hidden behind closed doors, whispered about in dark alleys, and rarely acknowledged. And for me, it is also one of the most tragic stories of all.

Order Book 2 Now

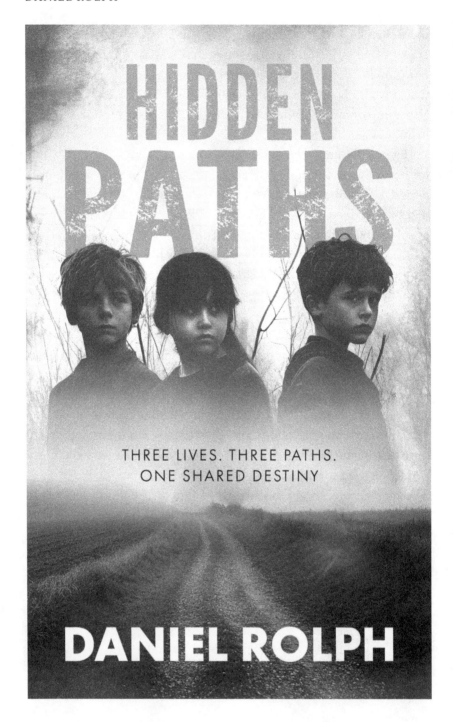

AFTERWORD

Thank you for joining me on this emotional journey through Shattered Paths. Writing this story was not just a creative Endeavor for me, but a deeply cathartic experience.

If you've connected with these characters, I hope you'll join me for the next book in the series, where we'll continue this incredible tale of survival through the eyes of another survivor.

You can follow my journey on Facebook and Instagram or visit my website at www.DanRolph.com

Thank you for being part of this journey with me.

Dan

ACKNOWLEDGMENTS

This book could not have come to life without the support, encouragement, and guidance of many people. To everyone who believed in this project and stood by me through the ups and downs of bringing this story to the page—thank you. Whether through emotional support, professional advice, or simply a kind word at the right time, your contributions have meant the world to me.

To the broader foster care community, and to all those who work tirelessly to give children a voice and a chance at a better life, your efforts are deeply appreciated. This book is for you, as much as it is for those whose stories often go unheard.

Finally, to the readers—thank you for taking the time to walk alongside these characters. Your willingness to engage with these stories, and your empathy, make all the difference